New Fiction

CHILDREN'S FUN FICTION

Edited by

Bobby Tobolik

First published in Great Britain in 2005 by
NEW FICTION
Remus House,
Coltsfoot Drive,
Peterborough, PE2 9JX
Telephone (01733) 898101
Fax (01733) 313524

All Rights Reserved

Copyright Contributors 2005

SB ISBN 1 85929 133 3

FOREWORD

When 'New Fiction' ceased publishing there was much wailing and gnashing of teeth, the showcase for the short story had offered an opportunity for practitioners of the craft to demonstrate their talent.

Phoenix-like from the ashes, 'New Fiction' has risen with the sole purpose of bringing forth new and exciting short stories from new and exciting writers.

The art of the short story writer has been practised from ancient days, with many gifted writers producing small, but hauntingly memorable stories that linger in the imagination.

I believe this selection of stories will leave echoes in your mind for many days. Read on and enjoy the pleasure of that most perfect form of literature, the short story.

Parvus Est Bellus.

CONTENTS

Title	Author	Page
Sullivan Diplock	Michelle Hinton	1
Future Boy And The Case Of The Missing Underpants	Linda Howitt	5
The Cat With Nine Lives	Barbara Russell	9
The Cottage In The Woods	Margaret Ward	14
Giant Bigboots' Christmas Present	Margaret B Baguley	18
Boris Bumble's Birthday Surprise	Beckie Royce	23
Red-Haired Rider	Natalie Holborow	26
The Adventures Of Philip The Field Mouse	Joan Peacock	31
Behind The Bush With The Mush	David Bilsborrow	33
A Boy And His Kite	C D Smith	34
Judy's Day At The Beach	Pauline Mayoh-Wild	39
King Monkey Tales	Christina Earl	42
Angel On The Top Of The Hill	Joyce Walker	45
The Enchanted Wood	Frank Howarth-Hynes	47
Charlie The Guinea Pig's Big Adventure	Mimie	52
The New Weapon	Jillian A Nagra	55
Jessica's Magic Umbrella	Doris Dowling	58
Peter And The Forest	Janet Middleton	60
The Oldest Christmas Present	Pamela Harvey	62
The Rainbow Teapot	Emma Lockyer	67
The Fox And The Curse	Susan Roffey	71
Granny Fry - Her Problem And Its Solution	A R Carter	79
Snowdrift	J Millington	81
On Suefari	Peter Asher	83
Princess Sugar	Patricia Green	88
Solved	Audrey A Allocca	90
Sam's Space Adventure	Hazell Dennison	95
A Wonderful Life	Gerard Allardyce	97
Betty's Mirror	Danielle Eyres	101
Mrs Prickles' Travels	Yvonne Peacock	106
A Holiday In Scotland	Elizabeth Love	109

SULLIVAN DIPLOCK
Michelle Hinton

No doubt everybody has heard of King Midas and how everything he touched would turn to gold. Well, I'd like to introduce you to Sullivan Diplock, he was a sweet ten-year-old boy and to look at him, you would have thought he was like any other ten-year-old boy. He had angelic features, beautiful big blue eyes and masses of curly blond hair. But unlike King Midas, everything Sullivan touched immediately broke. It was like he had some kind of curse hanging over his head.

Sullivan's parents had taken him to see many doctors to see if there was any medical reason why he broke everything with the slightest touch. Unfortunately, after many months of different tests, the doctors could find no medical reason whatsoever why he broke things, and they told his parents he was just a clumsy little boy and that hopefully he would grow out of it.

Poor Sullivan led a sheltered life, not because his parents made him live like that, but because he left trails of destruction wherever he went. The amount of money his parents spent replacing things that he broke was unbelievable. He had no friends and he never went to visit any immediate family. He had to have a home tutor for his schooling.

Mr and Mrs Diplock had a nicely decorated house, but they didn't have much furniture, just the basics. They had no nice ornaments due to Sullivan's condition, apart from one family heirloom; it was a figurine of a beautiful woman holding a little baby. From the day Sullivan was born it was drummed into him never, ever to attempt to touch the family heirloom. They had to watch Sullivan like a hawk, and they would cringe with trepidation at everything he would go to touch. But occasionally as Sullivan went to pick something up, he would stop and say, 'No, I don't want to pick that up today.' He had tried wearing gloves but in a matter of five minutes, the gloves would have holes at the end of the fingers. He could only wear elasticated trousers and slip-on shoes. If he were to put a pair of trainers on, the soles would drop off immediately.

One night, after Mrs Diplock had finished reading Sullivan his bedtime story, he was just nodding off when he had a secret visitor. He heard a really faint tapping on his bedroom window. At first he ignored it, then it got louder and louder. He sat up in bed, rubbed his eyes and stared at the little boy waving to him outside the bedroom window.

'Hello, my friend. I've been searching this neighbourhood for days looking for you. Oh, by the way, my name's Bosmite,' he said.

Sullivan sat mesmerised by the little boy who seemed to be floating on air.

'Sullivan, you are allowed to talk to me. Come here so I can make sure I have the right boy. But don't touch me, I don't want anything broken!' said Bosmite, with a cheeky smile.

Sullivan slowly got off his bed and walked towards his window. 'Um, how do you know my name?' he said.

'Because I've been sent here to help you!' said Bosmite.

'What do you mean you've been sent to help me? And why are you floating?' stuttered Sullivan.

Bosmite burst out laughing and said, 'I'm not floating, I'm standing on ladders. I'm here to help you because I know you have no friends and you're very clumsy. Trust me Sullivan, I know someone who can help you.'

'Wha-wha ... what are you going to do?' he said.

'Firstly, close your eyes really tight and when I say jump, I want you to jump as high as you can.'

'I can't jump out my window, I will get hurt!' said Sullivan.

'I didn't say jump out your window, just jump on the spot. Trust me,' replied Bosmite.

Sullivan closed his eyes really tight and waited to hear the word 'jump'.

'*Jump*, Sullivan, jump!' shouted Bosmite.

Sullivan jumped, then his eyes shot open. 'Whoa, how did I get down here?' he said as he looked around his garden.

'That doesn't matter. Follow me!' said Bosmite.

They both started to walk round the garden and Bosmite stopped at a huge apple tree. 'Now listen to me, in a minute a secret door will open in the tree,' said Bosmite.

'A tree doesn't have a door!' laughed Sullivan.

'This one does, it's a magic tree. Watch!'

All of a sudden, a door appeared. Sullivan's face lit up with excitement. He kicked himself to make sure he wasn't dreaming.

'Come on then, matey, let's go and pay Tulip a visit,' said Bosmite.

'Who's Tulip?' asked Sullivan.

'My mum, she's going to cure you.'

They walked through the door and ended up in a brightly lit room full of colourful flowers. There were bottles of potions lined up on the shelves and sitting in the corner on a rocking chair, was Tulip.

'Hi Mum, I've finally found Sullivan. Here he is!' said Bosmite as he pushed Sullivan forward.

'About time, dear boy. Come closer Sullivan, let me take a good look at those hands of yours,' she said.

Sullivan slowly started walking towards Tulip, his palms felt sweaty.

'Hurry up boy, I'm not going to hurt you,' said Tulip.

Sullivan held his sweaty hands out. Tulip grabbed them and studied them for about ten minutes. 'There's the problem. I've got just the cure for you. Bosmite, will you pass me the bottle marked 'Spindleweed' please?' she said.

'Oh no, Mum, don't use that one again. It smells nasty,' said Bosmite.

'Well son, that's the only one that will cure Sullivan, so will you please pass me the bottle?' said Tulip.

Bosmite passed his mum the bottle. She opened it and out crawled tiny, tiny spiders. Sullivan didn't dare move a muscle; he hated spiders.

'I'm now going to rub some of this potion on your hands and you will never, ever break another thing, and you will be cured,' said Tulip with a smile.

'Those spiders won't crawl on me, will they?' asked Sullivan.

'No, don't be silly, they don't like humans.' She then poured some of the gooey yellow slime onto Sullivan's hands and rubbed it in vigorously. Tulip was oblivious to the smell; both Sullivan and Bosmite heaved. 'There you go child, all done. Bosmite will now take you home and you must never tell a single soul about us, or the potion won't work,' said Tulip.

'Oh, OK then, well thanks anyway, but I don't think the potion will work on my hands,' said Sullivan.

'You will be surprised. Now off you go and get some sleep,' said Tulip.

Bosmite led Sullivan back to the ladders. 'It was really nice meeting you Sullivan, and good luck,' he said.

'Don't I have to close my eyes this time to get back in my room?' said Sullivan.

'No silly billy, just climb the ladders. Goodbye friend,' said Bosmite.

'Will I ever see you again?' asked a teary eyed Sullivan.

'Afraid not, we have to move on now to help more children. Take care,' replied Bosmite.

Sullivan climbed the ladders and he was just about to turn round and say goodbye to Bosmite, but he had already vanished. He leapt into bed and fell into a very deep sleep.

The following morning, Sullivan ran downstairs and headed straight for the family heirloom.

'Sullivan, don't even think about it,' said Mrs Diplock.

Sullivan wasn't listening to his mum. He clasped his hands around the figurine.

'Sullivan, *noooooo!*' shouted Mrs Diplock. But she was too late, Sullivan was already holding the family heirloom, and it didn't break. His parents couldn't believe what they saw.

Sullivan Diplock had been cured, and to this very day, he has never breathed a word about his friend, Bosmite, or his secret visit to see Tulip.

FUTURE BOY AND THE CASE OF THE MISSING UNDERPANTS
Linda Howitt

When Michael woke up on Tuesday morning, he had no idea of the predicament he was about to face. Had he known what was about to happen, he might have decided to stay fast asleep, but he didn't know and he did get up and that was when the trouble started. His underpants were missing!

What made this particular problem especially difficult was the fact that Michael could not tell his mum about the loss, not only because she would be extremely annoyed with him for losing an item of clothing, but also because she had no idea of his true identity, his secret alter ego. For Michael was no ordinary boy. He was a boy with a secret. A boy with a covert mission in life that not even his friends knew about, much less his mum. Michael was *Future Boy*.

Unfortunately they weren't just any old underpants that had gone astray. Oh no. He had any number of green, blue and even washing-mistake-pink pairs of underpants, not to mention those horrible ones with the purple dinosaurs on. He wouldn't have minded losing *them* but they were still in his top drawer. He had lost the ultra-special tartan pair. The super-duper ones that when worn over his yellow super-suit would let him see into the future, so that he could organise his crime-busting activities neatly around his school work. Not only that, his tartan underpants had yet another, even more important function. More important than crime-busting, more important than homework, and even more important than not scrunching sticky chews into the thick, fluffy, shagpile carpet in Mum's bedroom. These pants were very, *very* special indeed. They stopped farts.

It's true! Even the biggest, loudest, smelliest and most disgusting of pant-poppers could not get past these babies. Not even the ultra-silent, creep-up-behind-you-and-choke-you-into-oblivion kind stood a chance against them. They were impenetrable. In fact, they were so effective they could even stop the parps of people standing close by. You don't believe me? Well, think about this. Have you ever wondered why the Queen, film stars and celebrities never, ever seem to 'toot at foot'? It's very simple. They wear tartan knickers. In fact, the only people who don't wear tartan knickers are the big, beefy Scotsmen in their whirly, twirly kilts, who toss cabers and growl 'Let the wind gang free' because they are big and tough and not afraid to blow out in public. Michael was almost as brave as this, but he had to keep his mother sweet, not to mention the seeing into the future function that he had never found with any other underpants. His underpants weren't just special, they ... were ... incredible ... and they were missing.

As if matters weren't bad enough already, it was now 8.17am and Michael had to leave for school at 8.45am. That gave him just under thirty minutes to find his underpants. Where on Earth could they be? The possibilities were endless. What if Neville McBreville was on the loose again with his evil toaster set to incinerate? Michael's underpants were toast! Worse still, what if the school bully Genghis McGonagall had them and was, even now, planning the ultimate super-wedgie on Michael's arrival at school? The whole scene was too horrible to contemplate. He had to find those pants.

Just then, Michael's mum shouted him for his breakfast. Oh no! Just his luck. Now he would have to go downstairs and eat breakfast before he could look for his pants. He quickly got dressed and ran down to the kitchen. Twelve gulps, a slosh and a gloop later he had finished his frosted flakes and his glass of milk and was racing back up the stairs, two at a time, to his bedroom.

It was 8.34am. Not much time left. Now, where to start? Under the bed? He lifted the edge of his covers up to peer into the gloom beneath his bed and recoiled in horror. In amongst all the boxes of toys and his collection of odd socks nestled a large, green, fuzzy creature.

'Oh, excuse me,' said Michael, regaining his composure, 'have you seen my underpants?'

The fuzzy thing didn't answer, nor did it move and Michael began to wonder if it was alive. Was it perhaps plotting to leap at his face if he should dare wriggle under the bed? He decided to poke the fuzzy thing, but rather than risk having his fingers munched off at the elbow, he decided to do it with the end of a golf club to see what happened. Slowly, carefully, he reached under the bed with the club and gently prodded at the thing which promptly rolled over to reveal that it was, in fact, an apple that he had forgotten to retrieve when it rolled under the bed several weeks before. In the heat of a warm summer it appeared to have grown a rather wild and woolly green coat. Yeuch!

Next Michael decided to try looking behind his chest of drawers. Down there he found a model spaceship, a 20p coin, a miniature cowboy, three marbles, two metres of yellow wool attached at one end to a Spiderman, a playing card and lots of dust. But still no underpants. There was only one place left to search. Michael turned slowly round and looked up at it fearfully. The toy cupboard. Not even his mum in one of her *'I need chocolate now'* moods was *this* scary. In fact Michael could not actually think of anything that had ever been quite as intimidating as his toy cupboard. It was crammed full with toys, games, footballs, skateboards, books and jigsaws, all of which threatened to descend on him if he dared to open the door so much as a smidgen. Michael sighed at the thought of the mess he was about to create and the look on his mum's face when she saw it. This was not a job for the faint-hearted and not a job that should be tackled five minutes before leaving for school, but he absolutely *had* to find those underpants so that he could see into the future again and plan his superhero activities properly.

Then it hit him. Of course. Why didn't he think of it before? All he had to do was to think back to the last time he was wearing the amazing underpants and remember what he had seen in the future while he was wearing them. It was so simple. Now think ...

He had them on ... last night! Good start. Now what was he doing? He was ... doing his homework. Great, now he was getting somewhere. Now, what had he been thinking about? This was more difficult as his attention tended to wander a bit when he was doing boring old school work. Think very hard. He was doing number work, adding and subtracting, multiplying and dividing and wondering if he would ever use number work in a practical situation. Did his mum count all the socks into and out of the washing machine for instance? Well she *was* always complaining that all she ever got out of the machine were odd socks, even though she was putting pairs in. Wait a minute! That's it! He'd got it. He had thought about the washing machine, something that no ten-year-old boy ever thought about under normal circumstances, but Michael had and he had been wearing tartan underpants at the time. It was obvious. The pants were in the wash.

Oh no! This was a disaster. Washing his special tartan underpants was the mistake of the century. All that fabric conditioner spelled the end of any seeing into the future until the smell wore off and all that detergent would ruin the anti-fart coating. It would take at least six weeks to build that up again. The situation was dire. He had to act fast.

With lightning speed he raced back down to the kitchen. There wasn't a moment to lose, but his mum was in there. He had to get her out of the way if he was going to rescue his underpants and get to school on time. He needed a plan and he needed it now.

Furrowing his brow, he squeezed his eyes tight shut and concentrated very hard until he came up with something. Then, from his pocket he pulled out the yellow wool with the Spiderman attached and ran to the front door, sitting the figure just inside the letterbox. He then unravelled the wool carefully; this was not the time to have to start unpicking tangles. Sliding behind the long black coat hanging on the coat stand, he took care to make sure he was as fully hidden as possible and, crossing his fingers and closing his eyes, he took a deep breath and tugged sharply on the string. Spiderman flew from the letterbox making it clap loudly behind him. Pulling the wool quickly out of the way, Michael waited. Six point two seconds later, his mum appeared to answer the door.

As soon as she was past the coat stand he sped through to the kitchen and dived headfirst into the laundry bin. They had to be here somewhere. Trying not to think about what he was plunging through, Michael had almost reached the bottom when he found them, lying crumpled up between a pair of trousers and an itchy, bobbly, woolly sweater with fluffy bits that tickled his nose.

'Ah ... ahhh ... atchoooooooooo!' Michael sneezed so loudly and with such force that he was catapulted backwards out of the laundry bin and onto his feet just in time, before his mum reappeared with a puzzled look on her face. There hadn't been anyone at the door at all. It seemed the wind had been strong enough to clap her letterbox, yet when she looked out, there wasn't a breath of wind in the air. Very odd.

'Have a good day at school, Mikey,' she said, still puzzling over the door. She ruffled his hair on her way past and headed for the washing basket. Phew! He'd made it just in time.

'I will. See you later, Mum,' he said, grinning in triumph as he turned to leave for school with the prized tartan underpants safely in his pocket. And with their safe return to his possession, he also knew that in the future he would have to be a little more careful about where he left them.

THE CAT WITH NINE LIVES
Barbara Russell

Brownie was a beautiful chocolate-brown Persian cat with large orange eyes. He had two brothers and two sisters. When they were born, their mother rejected them. They were put into a cardboard box and taken to the animal sanctuary. Brownie's two brothers were all black. One was called Sooty and the other Smokie. His two sisters were Dolly and Duster. They were also brown, with a lot of black on their faces and legs. The kittens were fed regularly on bottles of baby milk because they had no mother to feed them. When they were eight weeks old, they were put in a large pen.

Anyone who was looking for a kitten would visit, and look to see if they were suitable. Even at that age, Brownie had a long, flowing coat. His brothers' and sisters' were not quite so long. Although he was the bonniest kitten of them all, they all found a home before him. His long coat put people off. They knew he would need a lot of brushing and grooming. So one at a time he watched them leave, until, finally, he was left in the pen all by himself.

Brownie was feeling very sad. He missed his brothers and sisters very much. He was tired of people admiring him through the bars, and then going home and leaving him. It was then that he decided on a plan. When Betty came round in the morning with breakfast, as soon as the pen door opened, Brownie was to make his escape. He had nowhere to go, but that did not seem to bother him. At least he would be free, and someone might be kind enough to take him in. He settled down comfortably for the night, so that he would be ready for what he had in store the next day.

It was the sound of doors opening and closing that woke Brownie. Betty was on her way round with breakfast. She was a kind lady and she loved all the animals very much. Brownie knew that first of all she would put a bowl of food in his pen, then she would turn her back to get the bottle of milk from the trolley to pour in his saucer. Although he was still very much in a daze, he remembered the plan he had made the night before. Patiently, he sat waiting for his door to be opened.

First of all, as usual, she gave him his food. Then, as she reached for the bottle of milk, he pushed the door wide open and scurried off down the corridor. He left behind him shrieks and cries. Betty was devastated. She could hardly believe what had happened. She was due to retire in two weeks time and she was going to take Brownie home with her because she had a soft spot for him. She had not taken him sooner because she did not want him to be left in the house on his own. By the time she had raised the alarm, Brownie was safely out of the building and breathing in the fresh summer air.

He did not know where he was, he just kept running across the fields as fast as his legs would carry him. After a while he came to a very busy main road. He did not know how dangerous roads were because he had never seen one. He had been in the sanctuary from being a kitten, so he did not understand danger. Before he realised, he was in the middle of the road. All he could hear was the sound of horns blowing, cars swerving and people shouting. The next thing he knew, he was lying on the side of the road. Fortunately, he had not been hit by a car, but he was overcome with panic and fear. A driver stopped and came over, which gave Brownie the force to get up and run. He was very exhausted, and starting to feel hungry as he had missed his breakfast. He learnt the hard way how dangerous roads can be and decided to try and find his way back into the fields. He would also have to learn how to catch his own food.

It was starting to get dark; he needed somewhere to curl up for the night. He came across a large haystack and he knew that was going to be his bed. He curled up, feeling very lonely, and wondered how his brothers and sisters were. He would have given anything to snuggle up close to them again. Instead, he faced the dark, eerie night alone, wondering what the next day would bring.

It was a bright, sunny morning. In the distance you could hear the cows mooing. That was the noise that woke Brownie. He had never heard it before and it startled him. All he could think of was food. What he would give for a bowl of Betty's breakfast. Instead, he had to go and find his own. Rather than cross the fields, he thought it might be safer to stay on the country lanes. It was a good thing he did, because eventually, he came to a little village. To his delight there was something sat on every step that he recognised from the sanctuary. It was a bottle of milk.

Brownie was desperate for a drink and something to eat. He rushed to the step and eagerly clawed at the bottle lid. As he did, the bottle fell over and smashed. He lapped as much milk as he could before the front door opened and a woman came running out shouting. There was milk and glass all over the floor. Brownie was eager to escape and he ran through the broken glass. He was limping badly on his front leg because he had cut his paw. When the woman was out of sight and he felt safe, he sat down and licked his paw to try and stop the bleeding. He then carried on a bit longer, when he came to a gushing stream.

Things were not looking too good for this hungry, homeless cat. He lay down exhausted by the stream, dangling his paw in the water to ease the pain. For a few moments he felt better and began to relax. Then all of a sudden, he heard a snarling noise. As he turned, he came face to face with a large wolf-like dog. With the shock of seeing this angry animal, Brownie lost his balance and fell into the stream. Within seconds he was floating away at quite a speed.

The next thing he remembered was waking up on a grassy bank with two excited children looking over him. The beautiful Persian cat had turned into a sopping wet, scrawny moggy. One of the girls went away and returned pushing a doll's pram. Between the children they managed to lift Brownie and carefully place him in the pram. He did not have the energy to run away. He also had the feeling that at last he was being cared for. They excitedly pushed the pram home, wondering what sort of welcome they would get from their mother.

Mrs Harrison was not an animal lover at all. She made it crystal clear to the children that as soon as the cat was well, he had to leave. They were very upset, but they were also happy that they could spend time with Brownie while he was recovering.

First of all he was dried with towels. Then they finished drying him with the hairdryer. A lot of time was spent brushing his beautiful coat. When all this was completed, he was given a saucer of milk and the leftovers from the evening meal. The children found a large box and lined it with blankets. Brownie was more than happy to curl up in his new bed after such an eventful day.

The next morning the children were busy getting ready for school, but they made sure their new friend was given a good meal. When they left for school he was left alone with Mrs Harrison. He did not feel comfortable with her and she would not let him move out of his bed. She threatened him with what would happen if he did. She would constantly shake the broom at him. He was longing for the children to return home so he would get some affection. As soon as they came in they would argue over who was going to cuddle him first. Neither of them knew the way he was being treated during the day.

This went on for some time, then, finally, he decided to be brave. He was not going to sit in that bed all day, he was going to please himself. Mrs Harrison had different ideas. As soon as he made a move she started waving the broom about. For the next twenty minutes he was chased around the house. The more he ran, the more angry she got, until finally she caught up and struck him with the broom. That was the last straw for Brownie, he knew he had to get away. The thought of not saying goodbye to the children was very sad, but he knew he would be gone when they returned. When Mrs Harrison opened the door to take out the refuse, the frightened cat was right behind her.

He had no idea in which direction he was going. All he knew was he had to keep on running. In the distance he could hear the sound of children's laughter. His legs took him in the direction of the noise. He ended up in a large playground full of boisterous children. They all gathered round to make a fuss of the very lonely cat. He was hoping that somewhere amongst them were his two friends that had rescued him from the stream. The children were eager to share their milk and crisps with Brownie, but suddenly his appetite had gone. The whistle was blown, the playground emptied and once again he was left alone.

Memories of his brothers and sisters kept coming back. Were they happy or were they finding life a huge struggle like he was? If only he could find his way back to the sanctuary. He longed for safety and someone to take care of him.

As he was leaving the playground, a huge white cat sprang from the bushes, his back was arched and he viciously attacked the helpless, brown fluffy cat. The only hope that Brownie had was to run up a telegraph pole. He had most certainly used up his nine lives. Now the terrified Persian was stuck at the top of the pole. People started to gather, afraid for the frightened cat. A man made a call to the fire brigade. The fireman attached the ladder to the pole and up he went. The cat was secured in a box and carried down.

The fireman said to his companion, 'I am sure that cat is on the front page of the newspaper.' The paper was on the dashboard of the engine. The story described how Brownie had escaped the sanctuary, and Betty had offered a five hundred-pound reward for his return. The fire officer rang Betty and she cried with joy. He was taken straight to Betty's house where a fur-lined bed was waiting for him, and more food than he could hope for. The other surprise he had was to find his sister Dolly in the same house. She had been returned to the sanctuary because she could not settle. Betty had taken her home. Brownie and Dolly had never been happier, they would never be parted again. Betty and the fireman decided that the reward should go to the animal sanctuary to help to feed the other animals until they were fortunate enough to find a loving home.

THE COTTAGE IN THE WOODS
Margaret Ward

It was four o'clock in the afternoon as the three friends headed towards the woods. James was ten years old and a bit of a rebel, Lucy was eight, a quiet child who enjoyed doing anything, and Suzy, who was eleven, was a bit of a tomboy. The three children played a lot together and enjoyed each other's company. James wasn't bothered that he was the only boy, because Suzy enjoyed climbing trees and doing the things that boys liked doing. Today they had all decided to investigate the woods. At school they had a nature table in the hall that was a little bare, so they thought that they might be able to find things for it in the woods.

'Maybe we will find a birds' nest,' said James as they walked between the trees.

'We might,' answered Suzy, 'but it must be empty and not being used, we could look up into the trees for one.'

With food and drink in rucksacks on their backs, it meant that they had all day together and they were very excited about what they might find for the nature table.

'It's a bit scary in the woods isn't it?' said Lucy.

'Don't be a baby, Lucy,' said James, 'you are safe with us and you know we won't leave you alone. Anyway, it's going to be such fun looking for all the things for the nature table.'

Putting her trust in the two elder children, Lucy seemed happy with James' answer.

'Lucy, you can look for any nicely shaped leaves that have fallen off the trees. Mum says that we might find some conker cases, but if we do to be careful because they are prickly on the outside,' Suzy told Lucy, suddenly feeling very much in charge of things.

As Lucy walked amongst the trees, she picked up some moss which was very soft and cushiony to touch and an assortment of leaves that had fallen to the ground. A lot of the leaves were brown, but a really nice shape, so she put them into her bag with the moss. There were plenty of birds flying amongst the trees, but the children couldn't find any nests yet.

Continuing to walk through the woods, James suddenly looked up and called out to the girls, who were a little way behind him, 'Look at that over there - it's a little old cottage. I wonder who lives there,' he said.

'Shall we go and have a look?' said Suzy. 'It looks a very old place, who would want to live in a place like that?'

'I don't want to go,' said Lucy, sounding scared.

'It's OK,' said James, 'no one will hurt us, we will stay together. We aren't doing any harm, we are just looking, and Suzy, it might be very old but it's a very pretty cottage.'

Reluctantly, Lucy held back behind the other two, so Suzy took hold of her hand. 'Come on, Lucy, stay with me,' Suzy said in a reassuring voice. 'You're right James, it is a very pretty place.'

As they approached the cottage they saw a very neat and tidy front garden. It had flowers growing in rows in the beds around the lawn and a little white wooden fence surrounded the cottage. Going through the front gate, the children walked along a path made of cobblestones. The front door of the cottage was made of wood and had a knocker shaped as a garden gnome. There were two little windows each side of the door with pretty curtains hanging on the inside.

'Shall we knock?' asked James. 'It's very quiet around here.'

'No,' shouted Lucy, becoming very frightened.

'Let's just look in the windows,' said Suzy. 'Oh, look in here, this room must be the sitting room, there's a fire alight in the fireplace and comfortable chairs around it, and there's a table and chairs over there.'

'Look in the window,' said James, 'there are toys everywhere, and look at those big teddies and dolls. I can see a train set over there, look! The train is going along the track on its own; the engine is pulling five carriages.'

James and Suzy hadn't noticed that Lucy wasn't with them. While they had been so engrossed looking in the windows, Lucy had made her way bravely to the back of the cottage. They suddenly heard an excited scream coming from her. Rushing around to the back of the cottage, James stood laughing, for in the back garden he saw Lucy standing in the middle of a miniature fairground. There was a big wheel going around on its own and clockwork people walking about. On the other side of the garden were toadstools and gnomes; some of the gnomes were fishing in the little pond.

'Oh my goodness,' said Suzy. 'What a lovely place this is, but I wonder who it belongs to.'

'There's no one around,' said James, 'but these clockwork people are walking around the fair and the train inside the cottage was going along on its own, it's all a bit strange isn't it.'

'Yes it is,' replied Suzy, 'and what about the fire burning in the grate? Someone must have lit that.'

'It's funny that we haven't seen this cottage before when we have been playing in the woods,' said James.

As the three children were looking and taking in all the events that were happening in the back garden, they suddenly heard voices approaching. 'Sssshhhh,' whispered James as he peered around the corner of the cottage, 'there's someone coming.'

'I'm scared,' cried Lucy.

'Sssshhhh,' repeated James. 'There are grown-up gnomes walking towards the front gate, it must be them who live here.'

'Don't be so silly James, you're trying to frighten Lucy. Everyone knows that gnomes can't walk, they are just garden statues,' whispered Suzy.

'Take a look yourself then if you don't believe me,' snapped James.

With that, Suzy peered around James and saw that what he had said was the truth. There was a man and woman gnome, the man had a white beard and moustache and the woman had a red and white dress on. They both wore red hats and had red shoes on their very large feet. The man gnome was pushing a wheelbarrow that was full of chopped logs, and lying on top of the logs was an axe. 'I don't believe what I'm seeing,' said Suzy.

'See - I told you so,' replied James, feeling a little bit smug.

'We have to get away and out of here before we are seen,' said Suzy.

'Yes,' said James, 'but wait until they both go in the front door, Mum won't believe this when I tell her what we have seen.'

'I'm scared,' cried Lucy.

'Oh,' said James, 'they have now gone in the door, now, ready ... *run!*' Grabbing hold of Lucy's hand, they ran as fast as they could, away from the cottage and out of the woods. Their hearts were beating loudly in their chests and Lucy was crying with fear as she was pulled faster than her little legs could carry her.

As they reached the edge of the woods, Suzy could hear her mother's voice, 'You'll be late for school, Suzy, if you don't get up now, what on Earth has happened to your bedcovers? They are all over the floor. It looks as though you've been having a fight with someone in your sleep! Now get up and come downstairs for your breakfast, you don't want to be late do you? I have been calling you for a while now,' said Suzy's mother.

'I think I've had a bad dream, Mum,' said Suzy, looking around the floor at her pile of bedclothes that were scattered.

'Never mind love, it's over now. Do you want to tell me all about it?' asked her mother.

As Suzy told her mum about the cottage in the woods, and about the gnomes living there and how the three of them had run away before the gnomes saw them, Suzy was so glad that it had only been a dream after all.

GIANT BIGBOOTS' CHRISTMAS PRESENT
Margaret B Baguley

Princess Cinderella's two children, little Prince Charming and little Princess Ella, were playing in the castle garden on a frosty morning in December when they saw the postman coming up the hill. As he came nearer, he slipped on a patch of ice and fell, upsetting all the letters out of his bag. As the children ran out to help him, their neighbour, Giant Bigboots came out of his gate and joined them.

'Why have you got so many letters?' he wanted to know as he helped to pick them up.

The postman, who was not hurt, turned to him. 'It's all these Christmas cards people send to each other,' he said and, looking through the letters, gave some to Ella to take in. 'Have you sent a letter to Father Christmas yet?' he asked as he turned to go, and laughed when Charming said they had. 'Well I hope you get all you'd like,' he called back to them as he made his way carefully down the hill.

Giant Bigboots looked at the cards and letters Ella was holding. 'What's all this about Father Christmas?' he asked.

'If you'd like a present for Christmas, you have to write a letter to him. I had a lovely big teddy bear last Christmas. He's so nice to take to bed and cuddle. If you bend down I'll tell you where to send your letter to, but be quick or you won't get anything.'

Two days later, at Reindeer Lodge, Father Christmas' gnomes went into their workshop and could not see out of the window. There was something white outside. They were just going out with shovels to move what they thought was snow, when fairies Rosebud and Daisy came in.

'It's not snow outside your window, it's a big envelope with funny writing on it. We'll help you to bring it in,' Daisy said. As they did so, Father Christmas came to tell the gnomes what work he wanted them to be doing that day.

'Whatever's this?' he asked as the fairies and gnomes brought in the giant envelope. 'Let's see what's inside.' The gnomes spread out the letter they found in it and in big scrawly writing, Father Christmas read:

Dere Farver Crisums
Plees can I have a teedy bur?
Luv from Bigboots.

'I'm sure he or she can have a - what did they call it? Teedy bur, but who is he or she and where do they live?'

Nobody seemed to know until Fairy Rosebud remembered something. 'My grandmother is a witch. She's staying with us until tomorrow. I'll ask her when I go home to lunch today, but I think it's the giant who lives in the big house at the bottom of the hill, near Princess Cinderella's castle.'

Everybody laughed at the thought of a giant who wanted a teddy bear, but Father Christmas said he should have one if they could make it big enough.

When Fairy Rosebud came back from lunch, she was able to tell Father Christmas all about Giant Bigboots. 'He lives by himself and has never had a Christmas present. My grandmother knows Bigboots' grandmother too. They'll be meeting next week when their friends have a Christmas party, so please, could Bigboots have his teddy bear?'

All the gnomes worked hard after Father Christmas told them to start on it as soon as they could, so the giant teddy bear was really fine when they finished it. It sat proudly in the workshop with one foot poking out of the door into the packing room. Nobody had thought of what would happen when they tried to move it or how Father Christmas could carry it on his sleigh.

When the time came to put all the presents into sacks ready to go on Christmas Eve, the head gnome was very worried. 'If we can't get that teddy bear out of the workshop, we can't pack the sacks,' he said and went to find Father Christmas. 'All the presents are behind the teddy bear, what are we going to do? We hadn't thought of that when we made it.'

Father Christmas asked if all the gnomes had pulled at the teddy bear together.

'We've tried it,' the head gnome said, 'it's no good, we're not strong enough and there's not enough room.'

They just stood looking at the teddy bear who stared back at them with his big glass eyes as if to say 'I'm not moving however hard you try' when Fairy Rosebud came down to get some sewing cotton for the last of the dolls' clothes.

'What's the matter now?' she asked and then looked at the teddy bear, still with one foot poking out of the workshop door.

'We've tried everything to get that bear out,' the head gnome told her. 'All the presents are in there behind him. We can't pack them in the sacks. What are we to do now? We only have three days left to get everything ready.'

Fairy Rosebud reached for the box of sewing cotton, took two reels and turned to Father Christmas. 'If I could go home now, I'll get Grandmother. She's sure to know what to do.'

'Go at once,' she was told, so after running upstairs with the sewing cotton, she came rushing down again in cloak and hood and out she went into the falling snow.

The time she was away seemed like hours and when the snow began to fall faster and thicker, they were afraid she had lost her way. Rosebud had reached home after battling through the snow only to find that her grandmother had decided to leave earlier to go to her friend's house. 'I've got to find her,' she'd told her mother. 'Father Christmas is in trouble and needs her help. Which way did she go? She may find it hard to get along in all this snow even in a sleigh. I've just got to try to stop her before she gets too far away.'

'Well take care, dear,' her mother said, pointing out the way where faint marks could still be seen; but Rosebud had gone.

The sleigh marks were faint and she became tired with walking in the thick snow when she heard a voice calling to her and a big white bird flew down. It was Harry Herring Gull who had been out fishing and was on his way home. 'Whatever are you doing here?' he asked.

'I've just got to find my grandmother because Father Christmas is in trouble and needs her magic to help him,' she told him.

'Can't have that. Hop onto my back we'll soon find her,' he said and in no time at all they spotted her sleigh and Harry, having called out to her to stop, flew down beside her.

'Whatever brings you here?' asked Grandmother as Rosebud climbed down from Harry's back.

'Father Christmas is in trouble and needs your magic to help him. Please come back with me. I'll tell you all about it as we drive along, but please hurry as there are only three days left before Father Christmas leaves to take the presents on Christmas Eve!'

'I'll go to see your friend and tell her what's happened,' Harry said, 'I know where she lives,' and he spread his great wings and flew away, after seeing Rosebud and her grandmother driving back the way they had come.

The snow had stopped and the moon shone brightly so they soon reached Rosebud's home and left the sleigh there. The gnomes and Father Christmas were delighted to see them when they came in at the packing room door.

'Now what's all the trouble with a teddy bear?' asked Grandmother, and laughed when she saw the huge bear with one foot poking out of the workshop door. 'If Bigboots wasn't such a kind-hearted, helpful giant,' she said with a twinkle in her eyes, 'I wouldn't do anything to give him such a fine present, but here goes.' Taking a red envelope from her bag, she stepped forward and sprinkled powder from it onto the teddy bear's foot. 'How small do you want him to be?' she asked, 'this is a grow small spell I'm using.'

Before their eyes the teddy bear was slowly getting smaller until the gnomes were able to pull him out of the workshop. 'That's fine for now, thank you,' Father Christmas said. 'Could you give me some of that to make him small enough to go in my pocket on Christmas Eve? But how am I going to make him big again?'

Grandmother opened a secret pocket in her bag and took out two packets. 'The red one makes things smaller and the green one makes them bigger. When you go to visit Bigboots, be sure you use the right one,' she said as she gave them to him.

'Will that powder work on anything else?'

'Yes, but don't let it get onto yourself or you could get stuck in a chimney with the powder in the green packet,' was her reply. 'Now I must be going as I'll have to be up early in the morning to start on the journey to visit my friend.'

'What about paying for the spells?' Father Christmas asked. 'You've saved me from having to take the workshop wall down.'

'Oh, nonsense, don't give me any money. Take it as a Christmas present,' Grandmother said as she went to the door. 'Remember what I said about those packets, that's all. Red one for small, green one for big. Goodnight,' and out she went, followed by Rosebud who was as amazed as everyone else in the packing room.

The gnomes set to work at once with packing the bags and, on Christmas Eve, Father Christmas set off on his journey round the world with Bigboots' teddy bear in his pocket with the two packets of spells.

He was careful not to mix them up as he slid carefully down the chimney of Bigboots' house and landed in his bedroom. Climbing up the bedpost of Bigboots' huge bed, he took the teddy bear out of his pocket and carefully put him at the end of the bed. *Now which is the right envelope?* he thought. *It's very dark in here.* Just then the moon came from behind a cloud and he was able to use the green spell. The teddy bear soon grew to his proper size and Father Christmas used the rest of the spell on a box of chocolates. *That should please Bigboots when he wakes in the morning,* he thought, as he drove away towards the castle to visit little Prince Charming and his sister Ella.

He was right. Bigboots was so pleased he wrote another letter to Father Christmas to thank him, but he never found out about all the fuss and the spell. That was a secret, only Father Christmas and all his helpers knew about.

BORIS BUMBLE'S BIRTHDAY SURPRISE
Beckie Royce

This is the story of a very lazy little bee by the name of Boris Bumble and his longing for a bright, new, shiny Prickallot sting. Boris lived in a hive called Uppatree Hanging. It was a very busy hive with lots of comings and goings, everybody always had something to do, mostly collecting pollen from all the beautiful flowers of the forest floor to make honey for the queen bee.

Now, Boris was a young and very naughty little bee, who did not like to go to school, especially if the sun was shining. Instead, he liked to play with his friends Barnabee and Buggabee, who also lived in Uppatree Hanging, in Honey Comb House. It was just below Honey Pot Hole where Boris and his family lived.

Mostly, Boris and his friends would fly about aimlessly in the midday sun playing bumble dabber, if they were not at school. This Boris enjoyed very much, but unfortunately, he was far too old to be playing with his friends and not studying, because when a bee gets to a certain age he is expected to go to the queen bee and collect his Prickallot sting. These are only given if a bee becomes mature and, in order to do, this he must first do lots and lots of hard work under the supervision of an older bee for three years. At the end of this, he has to pass a big exam before he then becomes a bumblebee.

Now, all of Boris' friends had their Prickallot stings, because they went to school and studied hard, but Boris didn't - he was far too lazy to listen and learn. Then one day, on his way home, Boris flew over to Sir Stingallot's workshop where all the stings for all the bees are made by Sir Stingallot himself. It takes a full three years to finish making a Prickallot sting! This is the length of time it takes to mature from a baby bumble to an adult bee.

As Boris began to read the notice on the closed door, which read, *Workshop closed due to birthday surprise,* Boris realised that he too should be proudly wearing his yellow stripes on his suit, and owning one of the most precious things a bee can own his Prickallot sting!

Boris began to cry as he realised that he was just about the only bee in Uppatree Hanging to have never owned a Prickallot sting; you see, it had never really bothered him till now. As he watched Sir Stingallot hard at work, he wished that the sting he was making was his, and he imagined the proud look on his father's face if he were to wear a sting as beautiful as the one Sir Stingallot was making. This made Boris very sad.

Boris decided that from that day he would go to school and study hard for the Prickallot sting he so wanted. He rushed home to tell his family, who of course could not believe their ears (well bees do have them you know), but the very determined Boris would not give up. He studied every day and sometimes long into the night and occasionally he even thought of going out to play bumble dabber, but he knew if he did this it would ruin his chances of ever owning his own Prickallot sting.

Three years of hard work went by and Boris could think of nothing else. Then one day, as he sat eating his yummy dewdrop lollipop on a branch of the old oak tree where he and his friends lived in the hive, Uppatree Hanging, he had an idea. He decided that because it was nearly his birthday, he would ask if he could have a party and invite all his friends, and see if maybe he could have his Prickallot sting early, but Boris' dad disagreed. 'No! Boris you may not have your sting early, but you can have a party.' Boris was very upset.

Boris wanted his Prickallot sting but his father insisted he must wait until the queen bee held a party in his honour. Poor old Boris was so upset that he sulked all day long. The next three days were terrible, Barnabee and Buggabee tried everything to cheer him up but they just couldn't.

Boris did not realise that the whole hive had already made plans for his birthday, including a big surprise! Of course they had asked the queen bee if it would be possible for Boris to have his Prickallot sting without her presence, to which she had replied, 'Yes, that would be fine, as Boris has worked very hard.'

The day of Boris' birthday came round very quickly and he was getting very excited at the thought of all his friends coming to his party. As they began to arrive, Boris noticed that they had all polished their Prickallot stings especially. Boris wondered why. At the party, everybody played lots of games including, of course, bumble dabber, as this was Boris' favourite game. There was lots of royal jelly and ice cream made from special flowers, and plenty of sweeties and honey sandwiches too.

Boris was having lots of fun, but he still felt sad because he thought he would not get his Prickallot sting. Then, all of a sudden, over the noise of the bees playing, his dad shouted, 'Hear me! Hear me!' and everybody stopped. 'It's Boris Bumble's birthday and we have a very special surprise from the queen bee for him for working very hard and passing all his exams. Come here and sit down Boris,' said his dad, then he put a blindfold over the little bee's eyes.

All of a sudden, Boris felt something very heavy being screwed onto his bottom. Everybody clapped as Boris stood up. As he did this, he felt very lopsided, but after a while everything was OK. He was so excited when he realised that of course it was the Prickallot he so wanted, that he buzzed round the whole room showing all his friends with a big smile.

That night, after all of his friends had gone home, Boris unscrewed his Prickallot sting so that he could go to bed (because, of course, everyone knows bees don't wear their stings to bed). Boris stayed awake for a long time just looking at his Prickallot sting as he could not believe the whole hive had known of his special surprise, and no one had said a thing. *How wonderful,* thought Boris, as he eventually fell asleep, happy and content, because Boris Bee was now a grown-up bumblebee.

Goodnight Boris!

A message from a bee!

Stings aren't meant to prick humans, oh no! It's just that if a bee lands on a human, because their Prickallot stings point downwards, they occasionally prick them purely by accident. Try to remember this next time you see a bee, as it could be Boris showing you his posh, new, shiny Prickallot sting.

RED-HAIRED RIDER
Natalie Holborow

Rosso was aware of the cold, almost threatening, silence that filled the house when he closed the door behind him. It seemed to skulk on the stairs, pace the length of the hallway, smile coldly at him from behind each varnished oak door. Resisting the urge to step back outside, Rosso hesitated at the doormat before letting his legs carry him into the centre of the hallway, a strong feeling of dread washing over him.

The eyes of many gold-framed portraits watched him with disapproval as his clothes dripped rainwater onto the polished hardwood floor, almost loudly against the silence that gripped the darkened hallway. No light filled the dismal rooms, no life seemed to exist in the stillness of antique objects and dusty artefacts that had been left on tables and window sills for years.

The sinister silence in the large old house was strangely familiar, yet Rosso knew he had never experienced it here. He knew it well, but it had only been around in the darkest moments of his past. Memories slipped from the darkest corners of his worried mind, of a silence that had terrified him to the point where his mind went blank and sweat poured down his neck. He remembered how he had cowered, waiting for a scream, a shout, or maybe a smash to break the soundless tension. Rosso chased the memories back to the depths of his mind. It was behind him now, he told himself firmly. It was nothing but a collection of bad memories.

Casting his dark - almost black - eyes around the room, Rosso knew something was different. Perhaps it was just the darkness of the rainy evening and the fact that the sunlight was strangled by a blanket of purple cloud. Perhaps it was the mixture of new and old about the house that confused him. Perhaps there was something he was unaware of.

'Mother?' The echoes that chased through the shadowy corridors frightened Rosso from the moment that he dared to speak. The silence terrified him, he knew that clearly, but it terrified him even more to break it with his own voice. It was as if he was challenging it, or maybe even betraying it.

The doors that stood in the walls almost called to Rosso, yet no light spilled from underneath any of them. Rosso knew this was strange. Mother hated the dark. To his mother, the darkness was almost like a curse or some disguise for a beast that lived in cold, empty places. She had been afraid of the dark for as long as Rosso could remember, yet she tried not to show it in front of her children. Her husband had used it against her, branded her a stupid, childish fool with a head so riddled with fairy tales that she was a step back from reality to everyone else. Rosso's mother had put on a brave face and pretended that her husband's words couldn't hurt her, but Rosso could see how much she hurt and it wasn't just words that Rosso's father had used to hurt Rosso and his mother.

'Mother, I'm home ... where are you?' Rosso stood, straining his ears for a reply to call back to him, a door to swing open and to see his mother standing with open arms for her son. But as hard as he tried to imagine it, the whole idea seemed wrong in the atmosphere that surrounded him. It was enough gloom to make flowers wilt and die, to stop the sweet sound of birdsong and to never believe that such thing as a sun existed. Rosso could only imagine thorns enclosing every door, ravens screeching from rafters and a heavy fog pressed against the floor to the ceiling for the rest of the days.

The door to the kitchen lay on Rosso's left and Rosso stood in front of it, scrutinising every crack, scratch and shape that was imprinted on its dark wood surface. His hands were frozen to his sides, making no effort to clutch the brass door handle or even tap on the wood. The silence seemed to deter him, whispering soundless threats in his ear and chilling his blood with the coldness of its breath down his rigid back. His conscience however, was trying to do the opposite.

Open the door Rosso, his mind seemed to surge, images of normality imploring him to reach out and grip the door handle. *You're a coward if you don't. Why do you fear nothing?* Rosso frowned, then realising that what his conscience told him could well be correct, reached out and touched the handle. Wrapping his fingers around the cold metal, another voice made him let go as if the brass were hot iron.

'Are you really daring enough to go in there at a time like this? I'd get out of the house if I were you, child.'

Rosso gasped with the realisation that the voice was not imaginary. It was a clear, commanding voice and turning, quickly, Rosso found himself staring into a pair of eyes as deep and green as the canals of this very city and a frown so concentrated, the eyebrows almost met. Rosso tried to shout or scream, but no sound would escape from his mouth. It was as if the silence had slipped down to his throat and melted his voice into nothing but gasping breath. The eyes that stared back at him sparkled with slight amusement but the strong sincerity was still visible as they gazed back at Rosso.

'Who are you?' Rosso managed to hiss, his eyes wide with fear and legs so numb he had to move his feet to ensure they were still there. The green eyes that captivated him with their distinct power hardly blinked and Rosso wondered if he was somehow communicating with a spirit.

'Is this the residence of Aida Porcelli?' The woman spoke with dominance, and for the first time, she pulled her eyes away from Rosso and examined the room with distaste, absently twirling a strand of long hair that cascaded like a vivid red waterfall to her hips. Rosso could see that she was not very young - perhaps mid-forties - but there was a clear sense of youth that seemed to radiate from her like rays of sunlight. She fixed her green eyes on a small painting on the wall and seemed to be slightly surprised. She slowly walked up to it and stroked a long white finger down the length of the frame. 'Interesting. Very interesting ...'

Rosso craned his stiff neck to see what she was looking at. It was nothing out of the ordinary, simply a painting of a waterside landscape in what looked like a vast forest; perhaps Canada. Hand pressed against her cheek, the woman pressed her lips with her little finger, obviously deep in distant thought. Rosso had time to observe her fully and wonder how on Earth the house had seemed empty (which was strange enough) and now a mysterious woman was here, uninvited, looking for Rosso's mother and marvelling over a rather ordinary painting.

Rosso's eyes watched her with both wariness and awe. She was swathed in a long, aquamarine muslin dress and on her hands she had a fascinating collection of carefully crafted silver rings and sparkling stones. On her neck hung a long chain with a silver feather pendant and she smelt slightly of his mother's floral perfume collection. For a good few minutes, she seemed unaware that Rosso was still in her presence and it was only when she saw him move to scratch his neck that she snapped round sharply.

'Do you speak, child?' she asked, a tone of impatience in her voice. Without having known her for any longer than a few minutes, Rosso predicted that this was a woman with a temper as fiery as her red hair. She stood in front of the painting as if worried that it might disappear if she left it.

'I - I do,' stammered Rosso, feeling his cheeks go red. Her powerfulness made him feel like a naughty three-year-old and it made him both respect and dislike her for it.

'Then answer me,' she said flatly, her eyes averting to the front door as if she were extremely bored. 'Does Signora Porcelli live here?'

'Yes, but she doesn't seem to be here at the moment,' said Rosso, then instantly regretted it. What if this woman wanted to see his mother for a bad purpose? Rosso felt guilt hit him like hands slapping him across the face. He sincerely hoped he had not got his mother into any form of trouble.

'Can you tell me where she is?' The woman picked up a photograph of Rosso in his school uniform, grinning stupidly and Rosso felt his cheeks redden again. He hated feeling so little and stupid, especially in front of women. He never knew what he was supposed to say to make himself seem tougher and more confident than he actually was and that only made his embarrassment worse. A small satisfactory smile stole across the woman's face as she observed the photo. 'You do look intelligent in this photograph, young man, I must say.'

Rosso's cheeks were by now practically on fire and, instead, he concentrated on her question to cool himself down. He hoped that she hadn't noticed. 'I don't know where my mother is,' he said in a voice so different, he hardly recognised it. It was supposed to sound cool and laid-back, but instead made him sound like an over confident little boy.

'Interesting,' said the woman, putting down the photograph. She fixed her eyes on Rosso and he looked straight down at his feet immediately. 'Does she often stay away from home so late?'

Rosso was aware that she was still watching him, almost as if she were reading him like a book whilst searching for the truth. Rosso tried to think of an answer, his mind riddled with confusion. It was as if all his thoughts were tangled in a great messy web and he found it too hard to focus. The woman sighed impatiently. 'She sometimes has to work late,' Rosso lied, 'or she goes to buy the groceries.' Neither of these excuses were true: Aida Porcelli was manager of her company and rarely, if ever did she have to work late. She would leave a message for Rosso at the door or perhaps telephone the school if so. Aida only ever bought groceries on the weekend when she was off work or her housemaid would buy them during the week.

The woman, who continued to stare at Rosso, looked very unconvinced. 'Indeed,' she said with disappointment and decided not to pursue the question any longer. She had been expecting this to happen from the very beginning, yet a foolish little voice in her mind had told her not to give up. She looked at Rosso; he certainly seemed very apt for what she needed. She only had to take another look at the school photograph to confirm her thoughts. She scrutinised him carefully; of course he could do with smartening up, but his tall, lean frame and those wonderfully dark, night-like eyes were definitely something that made him stand out. She recognised those nighteyes right away ... but Rosso had something very different in them ...

'Who are you?' Rosso asked, as it seemed as though the woman was trying to avoid the question.

Without warning, the woman leapt up as though someone had hit her and fixed her sea-green eyes on the front door. 'Quick - take this,' she said, pressing a cold metal object into Rosso's hand. She threw a hooded robe over herself and disappeared into the stone archway of the dining hall. 'I will return, Rosso!'

'Wait!' Rosso called, but the woman was running through to the back door and mounting her white stallion horse. Rosso looked at the object in his hand. His mother's silver ring.

THE ADVENTURES OF PHILIP THE FIELD MOUSE
Joan Peacock

Philip was a cute, little, furry field mouse. He lived at the bottom of the sheaves of corn in a tiny little nest.

The farmer had been very busy that day, tying up the corn with his special machine. Philip was very lucky to be alive, as the gigantic harvester had come along and bound up the corn. There was always plenty to eat in the cornfield. He munched away from morning to night on the ears of corn above his bed. His bed was very cosy and lovely and warm. In his nest, Philip had a table, a little chair and a tall cupboard in which he kept his teapot and his cup.

When it rained, Philip was able to catch some of the rainwater (especially on hot days) which, added to a couple of nettle leaves, gave quite a strong brew. If the weather was cold, the drink the little field mouse made was bramble tea, from some nearby berries. This was delicious and cooled Philip down before he began his afternoon scampering.

He loved to play, in and out, in and out of the sheaves of corn. It was on one of these excursions that Philip first met Sally Snail. Sally didn't need a nest or a house, because she carried a shell on her back, which was her home. Sally had a long, moist body and she could pull back into her shell if it was too hot or if it rained. She moved along the ground by creeping on a flat foot underneath her body. She made a slippery track and skated along it. Sally didn't need a teapot either as she drank droplets of water which collected at the base of the corn and ate leaves by scraping them with her rough tongue.

'Coming out to play?' asked Philip.

'Only if Luke can come too,' said Sally.

Luke was her little ladybird companion. He was a kind of beetle. He had hard, shiny front wings and was very brightly coloured. His body was red and his wings showed up as little black spots. He had cousins who were different colours. I think one was yellow.

'We'll go and look for Luke today then,' said Philip.

Sure enough, Luke was to be found on a neighbouring ear of corn. They had a little play. Luke flew about. Sally had a little slide and Philip had a quick chew on an ear of corn.

'You'll both have to come back to my place,' suggested Philip. 'I live in the next row of corn from here. You can't miss it. It is the one with the scarecrow. Come tomorrow at dawn,' said Philip, 'we'll have breakfast together. Corn and nettle tea and I'll get some leaves for you, Sally. For you Luke, do you like corn?'

Luke replied that he only ate aphids. That he was a good boy and liked to help the farmer.

'Well, aphids it shall be,' replied Philip.

The new day dawned. The red sun rose into a clear sky. There was a tapping at the door of Philip's nest. 'Come on in both of you,' said the field mouse, 'breakfast is served.'

Suddenly, there was the most terrifying sound. It was the farmer's machine coming to harvest the crops. 'You jump on my back, Sally,' cried Philip. 'We must run for safety.'

'I will fly,' called out Luke, 'see you in the barn.'

All three hastened to the barn for safety. Philip, clutching his teapot and Sally carrying the leaves and aphids in an old snail shell.

'We will be able to start a new life here, Sally. What about you Luke?'

Luke was so impressed by Philip's bravery that he announced that he would be very honoured to join them.

BEHIND THE BUSH WITH THE MUSH
David Bilsborrow

Deep in the forest, behind the old oak tree there lived little Impy, the cutest elf you ever did see. Impy often played with his two best friends, Snow and Grow. Snow was a bright red mushroom who always wore a green hat with a small bell on top. Grow was also red. He wasn't the brightest of mushrooms, he'd had to stay in mushroom school for an extra two years just to pass his two times table!

One day the three friends decided to go deep into the forest on an adventure picnic. They packed their baskets with all sorts of goodies and set off on their travels.

After walking for several hours, they came across a big bush in their way. 'What are we going to do?' said Snow.

'How are we going to continue our journey?' said Impy.

'I know,' said Snow, 'let's climb on each other's shoulders and climb over.'

'Good idea,' said Impy. Impy stood at the bottom and allowed Grow to climb on his shoulders. Snow then climbed up on both of them and jumped over the large bush.

A call of, *'Help!'* then came from behind the large bush.

'Oh no,' said Impy, 'how are we going to get over the bush, there are only two of us? If we climb on each other's shoulders we aren't tall enough to get over the bush.'

'I know,' said Grow, 'I will grow tall and then we can climb over.'

'How long will that take?' said Impy, looking baffled.

'Not long,' said Grow, who stretched and stretched and stretched.

Impy looked a little worried as Grow was pulling some very strange faces. 'Is it working?' asked Impy.

'No!' said Grow, who was out of breath.

'Oh, what are we going to do?' exclaimed Impy in a desperate voice.

After about twenty or so minutes of racking their brains for ideas, Grow jumped up in the air and shouted, 'I've got it, I've got it!'

Impy looked at Grow in amazement. 'What is it? What is it?' he quizzed urgently.

'Let's walk round it!' said Grow.

A Boy And His Kite
C D Smith

The sun was streaming down in noonday brilliance and it made everywhere feel like a cosy, warm kitchen. Beautiful puffy clouds floated on the horizon, giving an angelic quality to the entire scene.

Clemont McKenzie sat down on his verandah, lazily looking at trees and plants as they moved and swayed and waved in the summer breeze. He loved to feel the warmth of the day. He felt bored for a moment even as he enjoyed the sunshine and breeze and unforgettably lovely clouds. He always loved summer but this one seemed to have crept upon him and caught him unawares. He should have had plans, ideas and projects for the summer, he reflected.

As he sat on the verandah, more cool breezes blew by and gently prodded his mind until he thought of the perfect thing. He thought of making and flying a kite. To him it was no coincidence that there were gentle, cooperative breezes calling him to his new, temporary summer occupation: kite-flying.

Clemont, who was a high school student, decided that he would visit the town library as soon as possible to find a book about kites and kite-flying. In fact, he decided he would go there that very afternoon to find out what he could. He let his mother know that he wished to go to the library and asked whether she wanted him to buy anything for her. Mrs McKenzie asked him to buy a loaf of bread and a packet of butter only, and he was off.

On his way to the library, at the first corner, he looked up and saw a torn up kite which had been caught in the transmission lines and he remembered warnings he had heard on the radio about flying kites near them. *Well, it might destroy my kite too, that's enough warning for me,* thought Clemont. Finally, he reached the library.

He borrowed a book entitled 'All About Kites'. It was written by Cezan Manning, an authority on kites. The author wrote about the history of kites, ways of making them, how to make kites inexpensively, the dangers of kites, how to fly them and the different types of kites flown in different areas of the world. Clemont was especially interested so he read and read and learnt some important facts about kites. From an encyclopaedia, he learnt that kites are named after the kite bird, which is a graceful hawk.

On his way back home, Clemont stopped to buy cord, paper and masking tape for the making of a kite. He also stopped to find a short stick on which to roll the cord. As Clemont turned the same corner where he had seen the kite caught in the transmission lines, he noticed two boys, two of his friends, flying blue kites. He stayed with them for about half an hour and watched the two kites sailing and flying through the air as the breeze joined its strength with the boys to steer the kites. At times, the kites were held aloft in one position for long, magic moments as the boys held on to the controlling rolls of cord. At other times, pulled by breezes, the kites insistently went along some new path, some new tunnel of air and would nearly pull the boys along with them. At such times, they had to carefully, deftly, release the cords a little at a time, until once again, they were at one with the kites, the breeze and the land that surrounded them. It was a quaint and picturesque scene that any painter would love: two boys and their kites with another boy watching in awe, undulating countryside for a backdrop.

Clemont watched, mesmerized by the busy breeze as it had its way with the kites inasmuch as it could and the boys enjoyed themselves. Then he realised it was getting late and he had to hurry home but, before he did so, he told the boys that he was going to make a kite too. They were excited to see the materials he had bought after reading at the library. They had made their kites after watching others, without reading books, and wondered what Clemont's kite would be like. Roger and Winston said that they had to be going home too. They had to turn off the main road and go down a lane to get to their homes.

That night, Clemont was not his usual, quiet self. He was as excited as the other boys were about the kite that he would make and he wanted to make a sturdy, large one.

After supper, he asked his father to help him, first by cutting two slender pieces of bamboo to be the skeleton of the kite. The older man helped him to reel the cord onto the stick in preparation for flying the kite, while he listened to the tale of how the kites of Roger Gayle and Winston Jones had swung and swayed and swivelled in the wind earlier in the day. He was glad to help his son, who was usually a cooperative and well-behaved boy.

As Franklin McKenzie reeled in the cord from his son's hand, Clemont felt that maybe he himself was a big kite and his father was reeling him in. He felt secure with his dad and revelled in moments that were a companion experience to flying his kite. He felt that perhaps the older man was helping him to climb over an adolescent bridge in his own experience of growing up into the world of feeling at one with nature and working out the three-way tug of war that takes place amidst kite, breeze and boy, after a kite is born.

Mr McKenzie promised that the next day, as soon as he was home from work, he would cut the two pieces of bamboo needed and he would watch, and if need be, help his son to make his kite.

Clemont slept well after having shared his plans and activity with his father. He woke in good time the next day, looking forward to a day of work and play, or at least as far as the kite was concerned, the work being the making of it and the play being the flying of it.

In the morning, after his father had left for work, Clemont helped his mother make beds, sweep the house and water plants. Then he had to go to a nearby shop to buy the bread and butter he had forgotten to purchase in the town the day before. He was rewarded with some of the bread and butter, with drinks, for lunch and then, only then, did he get the chance to work on his kite.

From what Clemont had read and from what he had seen of the other boys' kites the day before, he realised he had to take several steps to complete the making of his kite. He spent the afternoon cutting and preparing his kite.

It was soon four o'clock and he looked forward to his father coming home to look at what he had already done and to cut the bamboo pieces for him. Now the kite was ready for the bamboo diagonals.

Clemont looked at his blue and red kite and again he felt like he himself was a kite, as large as his own kite, then getting larger and larger, as large as life. He felt conflict. He felt that perhaps rules and stipulations and obligations of home and school sewed him in, tied him down, limited him; while different experiences of growing up such as failing a test and being put in detention, losing a good friend, missing classmates who lived far away during holiday time or being told he did excellently in a class activity, seemed to open his feelings and his sense of pride, his intellect. Now he was tugging, then he was sliding freely. Now he was resisting, then he was gone with the wind. He sailed with abandon through cool breezes under a warming sun and saw the land get further and further away from him. He had never seen grasses and cows and hills and houses this way before. He flew and he viewed.

'You are ready for the bamboo now, man.'

Clemont heard the deep voice of his father and his laughter as the man stood over the kite with the cord in one hand and the two pieces of thin bamboo in the other. The adolescent sailed on the winds of consciousness, back through the semi-sleeping state of meditation, as his father's voice reeled him in.

'I'm going to give my kite eyes, wide open eyes so that it might see,' were the words with which the son greeted his father. To the son, he was fashioning the kite after his dream, maybe his eyes would be opened, to land and life and meaning. To the father, Clemont's eyes were being opened to technicality and to artistry and so, each satisfied with his own thoughts, they set to work together on the kite.

'You were fast asleep so I went to cut the bamboos,' the father said as he handed them over. The boy checked that they were the same size and thanked his dad. He handed back the bamboos for his father to shape and began to make kite eyes. Kite eyes were not like person eyes. They were not small eyes. Clemont made large eyes and placed corneas in the middle of them; he drew eyelashes and thick black eyebrows, all with a large black marker. The eyes stared back at the person who had drawn them and he laughed. His father laughed too and called Clemont's mother to come and look at the kite with eyes. She raised her eyebrows. They all looked at the kite eyes and loved the big, expressive kite. She chuckled, said it would soon be time for supper and reminded them that a kite might have eyes, but it was people who had hungry stomachs.

An hour and a half later, Clemont thought of see-saws in kindergarten as he sent the bamboo pieces through the cuts in the paper. He sent the bamboo up through a cutting, then down through the next, up through another cutting, then down into the next until the see-saw was over. Then he showed the kite, in its essential form, to his parents, who were reading the day's newspaper.

It was not long before the kite was ready and the kite-maker used a heavy amount of masking tape to make sure that the few bamboo ends were secured onto the paper and also not able to fall out from the cut openings. His father took more of a back seat now and watched him as he finished his kite by attaching a tail made from scraps of cloth.

Soon enough, the kite that had eyes was well-known to neighbours nearby who saw it on some of its journeys in the now slightly stronger breezes that blew. Clemont would stand on his verandah or outside with the reel of cord and slowly release his kite when the breezes were just right and his parents would watch him as the kite flew higher and higher until it was steady. Sometimes he had to return home, albeit gladly, when it rained.

At times, Clemont knew the feeling of oneness that occurred as he stood planted on the land, in control of the kite which moved against a backdrop of hills and houses and clouds to complete the scene. He revelled in being master of something of his own creation. He enjoyed this new activity that made him feel in tune with the summer and the scene all around him. The kite was the signal that he sent, of a new well-being.

JUDY'S DAY AT THE BEACH
Pauline Mayoh-Wild

Once upon a time there was a little girl named Judy. She lived with her mother and stepfather on a farm near the seaside and she was always very miserable. This was mostly because her mum was always keeping her away from school to help on the farm because her mother was not very strong and was always sick. Because of this, Judy missed a lot of lessons, so when the exams came around, Judy would always fail them. This upset her very much because she knew if she had not been away from school so much she could well have passed all the tests. The kids in the school used to call her names and no one befriended her so she became quite a loner.

One good thing about the farm was that it was quite near to the seaside. So at weekends Judy was allowed to go to the beach for a couple of hours each day (Saturdays and Sundays).

One day whilst Judy was playing on the beach, she heard a little voice. It said, 'Hello.'

She turned around but there was no one there. *Where could the voice be coming from?* Judy thought to herself. She carried on playing and again she heard the little voice.

'Come over here!' it shouted this time.

Again she looked around and saw no one. Then she decided to sit down and have her lunch which her mother had packed up for her.

As she sat on the sand eating her sandwiches, the sun came out and she could see something glistening on the beach in front of her. She walked over to it and saw it was a light yellow shell, quite a big shell. She picked it up and put the shell in her pocket to take home and keep it in her little box she kept in the drawer in her bedroom.

When she got home she did not tell her mother she had found the shell, she just went up to her room and put the shell in her little keepsake box. She went downstairs for tea and, after tea, she said to her mum, 'I feel tired tonight so I am going to bed early.' Really she wanted to have another look at her bright yellow shell.

After a while she put the shell under her pillow and decided to go to sleep. As she was dozing off she heard the little voice again …

'Hello.'

Judy jumped up in amazement. Where could this voice be coming from?

'I am under your pillow,' the little voice cried out, 'pick up the shell and look into it,' the voice said.

Judy quickly picked up the shell and gazed into it. She gasped when she saw a little boy inside waving at her.

'Hello,' he said again, 'what is your name?'

Judy was shocked but very excited. 'My name is Judy,' she said, 'what is your name?'

'My name is Cigam.'

'Where do you come from?' she asked the little boy nervously.

'I come from a very far away land,' said the little boy. 'I have noticed you on the beach at weekends and you are always alone. Why is this?' he said.

'I have no friends,' said Judy.

'Why?' said Cigam.

'It's because I am always staying at home on the farm to help my mother,' she replied.

'Why would that make you sad?' said Cigam.

'Because I cannot even read or write,' said Judy.

'I will teach you to read and write,' he said. 'Each night before you go to bed I will help you with the lessons you have missed at school.'

'That would be wonderful,' said Judy.

Every night Judy would go to bed before 8pm and she would have one hour lessons from Cigam. This lasted for about four months. Soon the sadness was fading from her face, she began to be her happy self again just like before she lost her father, and her mother noticed such a change in Judy. Then exam time came around again at school and all the kids were laughing at Judy as she handed in her exam papers.

'You may as well throw them in the bin,' said one girl, 'you are hopeless, you know nothing.' But Judy just smiled and ignored her.

When the exam results came out everyone in the class just sat there, stunned. They could not understand how Judy had become so clever. She had been the laughing stock of the school for so long, now everyone wanted to be her friend - kids could be so cruel.

Judy never told anyone about her yellow pebble or her little friend Cigam, she just smiled to herself and carried on with her everyday life on the farm.

When she grew up she became a lawyer and had such a good business, her mother was able to sell the farm and live in a beautiful bungalow by the seaside, which Judy bought for her and her stepfather. Her mother's health was better than it had ever been.

She kept the pebble until she grew up and was married, and then one day she went down to the beach and threw the pebble in the water, so that it might help someone who needed it as she had done when she was a little, lonely and unhappy child and very miserable.

She did not need it any longer as she had everything now and she was the happiest she had ever been in her life, thanks to Cigam, her little beach friend. But she never noticed that Cigam spelt backwards was *magic*.

KING MONKEY TALES
Christina Earl

Once upon a time there was a young monkey called Peeto. He lived on an island where only humans ruled. Monkeys were considered inferior and were caught to be sold as slaves. But Peeto was not just any old monkey; he had hopes and dreams, loves and hates - the mind of a human. His days were spent writing about his hopes for the future and the things he wanted to change. The humans would call these fairy tales, but for Peeto, they were his dreams and goals in life.

Peeto moved through the jungle more than once a week to keep away from the humans and to be safe. When he was young he had promised his mother to live how he would like to live, but to stay away from the humans. He couldn't remember much more about his mother, only her face of terror when the humans had caught her. But before they did she had hidden Peeto in the depths of the cave that was once home. Peeto had never met his father either, he had never even heard anyone talking about him, nobody seemed to want to tell him anything.

Peeto wished to find out answers and the only way of doing this was to break his promise and head toward the human village. Peeto had never made friends as he was scared that they would just get taken away and he couldn't handle the pain again.

He set off alone for the village, scared of what he might see, but also making a plan, then another, then another and then another. You see Peeto was a clever monkey; he always knew that every living thing needed more than one plan, because if one failed and you didn't have another then there would be no way out of complete failure.

As he was walking through the jungle he heard a scream. He knew what that scream meant and he couldn't ignore it. It would be stuck in his mind for the rest of his life if he did; he made plans and ran towards the shrieks of terror.

The humans had a young lady monkey cornered and were just then about to spring the net ... but Peeto had other plans. He jumped and ran with all his might and put all his strength into his arms and legs and tail. He sailed through the sky, pulled the lady monkey's arm and carried her out of harm's way before the humans could even blink. He then took her to the nearest cave and kept guard, to make sure the humans hadn't followed them.

The lady monkey's name was Joanna and she was very annoyed that Peeto had 'saved' her. She told Peeto to mind his own business and leave her alone. And then when Peeto asked her why she wanted to be caught, she fell to the floor sobbing, and that's where she stayed for hours. They were hiding in one of Peeto's old caves, you could always tell because of the writing all over the walls.

Joanna explained to Peeto that night why she had to let the humans take her. All of her family and friends had been caught and taken away the day before, and she loved them all dearly. She loved them so much that she would die for them, if it gave them a chance of survival and freedom.

So the next day they set off once again. But Peeto was unaware that the hunters had found the cave they were hiding in hours before.

The hunters found the writing on the walls, hundreds upon hundreds of stories and adventures. The hunters called out in alarm to the village. They believed that there was a young child lost in the jungle, all alone. Well the whole human population gathered in the jungle and spread out. Looking for the 'lost' child, they searched all day and night. But the humans were unaware that Peeto and Joanna had found their families and were helping them escape, giving them freedom.

Some of the humans began to tire, so they travelled back to the village and what they saw was unbelievable to them ... hundreds of monkeys free, running for their lives! Joanna screamed at Peeto to hurry, yet he was more interested in finishing his writing on the leader's house, telling the story of his life. And this was what got him caught. A hunter came up behind him, not at any fast speed at all, and caught him in a net. But the hunter then realised that the monkey was not just vandalising his house, but was writing, human writing, stories even.

He couldn't believe what was happening, what he was seeing ... and then Peeto looked into the leader's eyes and told him, in the human language, fully sentenced and pronounced perfectly, what he wanted to be changed.

The leader screamed, and screamed and screamed. *This must be impossible,* he thought. *Monkeys don't talk, monkeys can't write, monkeys don't think* ... Then the leader's wife opened the door to see why her husband, all brave and mighty, was screaming. When she found out why, she smiled and laughed and explained to her husband that she gave Peeto permission to write on the house.

The leader was shaking and the other humans gathered around. But instead of catching Peeto, they crowned him their new leader, King Monkey, leader of the humans. And then everything changed.

Monkeys lived free, safe and happy, no longer imprisoned by rules and work. They could live life by their own accord, have families again and smile again. Peeto met his long-lost father and built a house for his parents near his own. And of course, there was a big party in honour of the new leader, King Monkey and to celebrate his marriage to Queen Joanna.

That was the first legal monkey marriage since before the humans came to the island. And of course afterwards, there were many more. And for Peeto, King Monkey, leader of the humans, all his dreams came true.

Angel On The Top Of The Hill
Joyce Walker

Tomorrow I'm going to climb to the top of the hill. I'll leave early, as soon as the dawn breaks, before my mother can stop me. She says it's dangerous because the path is very slippery and many people have fallen while trying to reach its summit, but I don't care, I'm going to climb it anyway.

The doctor tells me it's dangerous too. He says my legs are too weak and my heart isn't strong enough, but I don't care about that either. I'm tired of lying here in my bed, reading books from kindly relatives who shake their heads sadly and whisper behind closed doors that I'm not long for this world.

Think I don't know I'm dying? I talk about Christmas and the presents I'd like and they promise me everything, though they know as well as I do, that, unless there is a miracle cure, I won't see it. I'm not afraid, but I'd like to do something before I have to go. My friend told me that on the top of the hill there's an angel who might be able to make me better, she says she's seen him. I'm not sure I believe her, but if it's true, all the more reason to go and if not, what is there to lose? I'll show them all that I'm not afraid. I'll show them that I'm not weak. Tomorrow I'll climb to the top of the hill.

It's morning, cold and bright. I put on my coat and walk out into the crisp air. The wind takes my breath and I have to stand by the gate for a few minutes. I'm frightened that I'll be discovered but the curtains in my parents' room remain firmly closed and, though a dog in a nearby house barks, nothing else stirs.

At last I can breathe again and I walk slowly to the end of the street. I want to run but I must conserve my strength or I won't make it to the bottom, let alone the top. I can see the hill now, but I can't see the angel for the sun stings my eyes and makes me squint. When I get to the foot of it I'll rest for a while. Then I'll show them I'm not afraid. I'll show them that I'm not weak. I'll climb to the very top of the hill.

At first it's not too difficult, for the incline's very gradual, but when I'm almost halfway up it gets steeper. My legs ache and my head. Perhaps I should go back, but I look up and tell myself that if I can walk the same distance again I'll be there. I stagger on, dizzy with the effort of putting one foot in front of the other, and will myself to keep moving. I still can't see the angel. Perhaps, after all, he doesn't exist.

Perhaps I should have stayed at home in bed with my books and all those knowing smiles. Perhaps ...

A piece of rock crumbles beneath me, I slide down a few feet, grazing my knees. The pain makes me bite my lip. I taste blood and reach out with my hands, searching for something, anything to hold on to that will break my fall. A rocky outcrop, a tree, a branch, another human being. I lose more flesh from my knees and my hands are red raw. I cry out but there's no one to help. I am falling, falling, falling, down, down, down.

On top of the hill stands a black-cloaked figure. He's been watching the girl for some time. He runs down the hill and calls out to her. 'Jenny, take my hand, I'll help you. We'll climb to the top together.'

The man comes from nowhere. I take the hand he offers and stop falling. He's very strong and I'm soon on my feet. I don't hurt anymore. My hands and knees are completely healed and I feel strong again, stronger than I have done for a very long time. To the peak, up, up and up. My dark-clothed companion and I run.

At the top of the hill I turn and look down into the valley. Somewhere down there is my parents' house. I know I'll never go back, but I don't mind. I stand there and shout, 'See, I've made it. I knew I would. I've found my angel and he's made me better.' I look into the man's kind face, 'You are an angel, aren't you?'

'Yes, I'm an angel, a very special angel, and I've come to take you to your new home.'

At the top of the hill there's a large black stone, Angel's Rock, the locals call it. When they found Jenny's body she was leaning against it as though resting before her journey back. And as they looked into her cold, dead face, they were surprised to find that she was smiling.

THE ENCHANTED WOOD
Frank Howarth-Hynes

'One day, in the Enchanted Wood, pixies and elves were playing on the bank of a babbling brook. They had been out most of the day, collecting toadstools, which is their basic diet. Now their baskets were full, they decided to have a rest and a little playtime before setting off home. 'It's getting late,' said the babbling brook, 'it's getting late.' The little singsong, tinkling voice from the brook reached the pointed ears of the pixies, who at first were too busy at play.

'Ooooh, we'd better set off back, it'll be dark soon,' said one frightened Pixie. They all thanked the babbling brook for the warning, and picked their baskets up ready for home.

They had only just began to make their way into the wood when they heard a roar, that only a dragon could make. All the pixies froze in fear, the dragon roared again in anguish, followed by the most pitiful, mournful cry the pixies had ever heard. Then without warning the dragon appeared as if from nowhere, looking down at the frightened pixies. 'Wha ... whatever's the matter?' said one pixie, who managed to find his voice.

'Please don't hurt us,' squeaked another pixie, 'look you can have all these toadstools.'

The dragon looked down at the toadstools in distaste. 'I don't wish to hurt any fairy folk, if I've frightened you, I'm sorry,' said the dragon in a deep baritone voice, which scared the pixies even more and to make matters worse, the dragon released two giant teardrops, that drenched them all.

'Ooooh,' squeaked the pixies, scattering briefly and then regrouping, once again.

'Why are you so sad Mr Dragon?' asked one of the pixies.

After a long pause the dragon answered, 'Well, I don't know how it's happened, but somehow, I've lost my fire. No matter how I try, I can't breathe fire, watch, I'll show you.' Taking a deep breath and giving a mighty blow, the dragon blew and blew, but was only rewarded with two puffs of smoke. 'You see.' He began to blubber, 'No self-respecting dragon can live with that.'

'I have an idea,' said a chubby little elf, who sounded very positive, 'the Moonqueen will help.'

'The Moonqueen?' pondered the dragon. 'I've heard of her power, do you really think she would help?' he said with a faint glimmer of hope.

'I will help you,' came a disembodied voice. The dragon and all the fairy folk looked around fearfully, but could see nothing. 'Don't be afraid, I am the Moonqueen, if I help you, you must also do something for me, but I must warn you to prepare for a very dangerous journey.'

'I will do anything to get my fire back,' said the dragon.

'Then listen carefully, all of you,' the Moonqueen continued, 'there is a golden amulet, that hangs from a tree at the edge of the swamp, it was stolen from the Land of Beyond long ago, and is said to have great magic power. You must travel to the Aurora, where the unicorns live, they in turn will guide you further, good luck,' and the Moonqueen was gone.

The silence was deafening, for a few moments, and then everyone seemed to talk at once, and all the pixies gathered round the dragon excitedly. Suddenly, a cute little fairy appeared from nowhere and said, 'I've been sent by the Moonqueen and I will take you to the Aurora. My name is Twinkle,' she said with the sweetest smile. 'Now there's no time to waste, follow me,' and off she went, a tiny little beacon of light. On and on she flew, slowing down now and again so everyone could keep up with her. Finally, they all came out of the wood, into a clearing, where the sun shone brightly. Twinkle stopped, and pointed, 'Look there it is,' she whispered. They all gasped in amazement, before them was this vapour of blue shimmering light, that changed shape and colour at the blink of an eye. 'This is the Aurora, don't be frightened,' whispered Twinkle with a smile.

At that very moment, one by one, the unicorns stepped out, snorting and shaking their heads pompously, each had a golden, spiralled horn on their forehead, which glowed with power. There were seven of them, and one of them slightly larger than the rest, trotted forward. 'I am the leader of all the unicorns, the Moonqueen has told us about your task and we are to guide you through the Dark, Angry Wood.'

'The Dark, Angry Wood,' echoed the pixies and the dragon.

'Why is it called that?' asked the dragon, with a puzzled frown.

'You will find out soon enough, it is a very dangerous place and only we can pass through in safety,' said the unicorn. The unicorns formed a circle around the pixies and the dragon. 'Do not leave the circle for any reason and you will be safe, now we must go,' commanded the unicorn. It wasn't long before they noticed a cold, icy mist, that quickly descended on them. Nobody in their wildest dreams could anticipate what would happen next, as everyone was taken by surprise by the wild movement of the trees. Their branches reaching out, like bony fingers, and they knew now, why it was called the Dark, Angry Wood, as every tree had an angry, snarling face and if that wasn't enough, monsters of every shape and size came out of the freezing mist. This place was truly the stuff of nightmares. Time and again, they tried to grab anyone careless enough to leave the circle. The terrible shapes shrieked and roared, showing razor-sharp fangs and claws, joined tirelessly by the angry trees, who by now, were in a frenzy of not being able to get through the magic shield of the unicorns. Slowly, ever so slowly, the circle of unicorns made progress and at last came to the end of the Dark, Angry Wood.

It was only then, that the circle broke. Nobody spoke for what seemed a long time. The leader of the unicorns was the first to break the shocked silence. 'You did well,' he said in admiration, 'but there is one more task that you must complete, you must keep on this path, and it will take you to the edge of the swamp, there hangs the amulet, but there is more danger. Three wicked witches are nearby and under their control is a giant raven, who lives in the tree next to the amulet.'

'Hmmm, how are we to get past the witches and this raven?' asked the dragon.

'Do you still want your fire back Mr Dragon?' asked the unicorn, ominously.

'Even more, now that we've all come this far,' said the dragon fearlessly. All the pixies and Twinkle jumped up and down and cheered in answer to the dragon's statement.

'Very well, the Moonqueen sends this,' and as soon as the unicorn had spoken, a small phial of green liquid appeared in Twinkle's little hand.

'Oooh,' she said in surprise, 'what am I to do with this?'

'Once again, you must all listen carefully, said the unicorn. 'This is the plan ...'

They had been on the thin, winding path that led into another part of the wood when cold, damp fingers of mist, once again, brushed their faces. Thankfully no monsters came out of it, not yet ... the dragon thought back to where they had left the unicorns and was reassured to know they were waiting for them. 'It's in there,' whispered Twinkle, 'look.'

Sure enough they had reached the edge of the swamp. They saw the witches stirring a large cauldron. 'Are we ready?' said the dragon in the lowest voice he could muster. They all nodded. 'Twinkle you know what to do,' but Twinkle had gone.

The witches were cackling round the cauldron, trying to conjure up new spells, when they all saw the dragon, at the edge of the swamp. For a few seconds you could cut the silence with a knife and then one of them spoke. 'Well, if it isn't Old Smokey,' and they all fell about rolling on the ground, cackling and screeching.

They know ... thought the dragon. 'If you don't stop your cackling, I'll burn you all to ashes,' roared the dragon in his most threatening voice. This statement made the witches even worse, as they held their stomachs in a frenzy of slavering and cackling. All this time, Twinkle was flying towards them, if they saw her now she was finished. When she was directly above them, Twinkle uncorked, and poured the phial of liquid over all three witches, and chanted the words, *'Begone from whence you came,'* three times. The witches realised, but too late, as they, and their interminable cackling, faded and disappeared, completely.

'Look out, look out,' warned the dragon as the giant raven swooped down, straight for the pixies, scattering them everywhere, but with their quicksilver speed, they weren't so easy to catch. The dragon moved forward to help them, but out of the corner of his eye, he saw something, that made him whirl round, to be confronted by the most nightmarish monster from the swamp. It moved towards the dragon menacingly. The dragon roared, he was just as big, and he wasn't afraid. With a mighty swish of his tail, he whacked the monster so hard, once, twice, until it disappeared beneath the swamp. Only a large circle of gurgling mud remained and then nothing ...

The raven was still busy trying to swoop on the pixies who proved they were much too fast, but at the moment the raven was not deterred. The dragon turned and saw Twinkle waving the amulet frantically, left and right, trying to draw the raven's attention away from the pixies. The raven saw the amulet in Twinkle's hand with its beady eyes and flew with a shriek of triumph towards her. As the raven swooped for the kill,

Twinkle began to rub the amulet, and chanted, *'Come from within - I command you - come from within.'* As she mouthed the last word, the raven landed, and became very docile, and then even stranger, the raven began to shrink, smaller and smaller, until finally, all that remained was a chubby little elf.

Everyone gasped in surprise at the sight of the elf, who ran over to the pixies, hugging them all, 'Thank you, oh thank you, at last I'm free.'

'What happened to you?' asked Twinkle.

'The witches captured me, long ago, and cast a spell on me, forcing me to be their servant, and guard the amulet.' The elf looked round, uncertain and with fear, at the steaming cauldron.

'You're safe now,' said the dragon, 'the witches are gone.'

'I think we had better go too,' said Twinkle, putting the sparkling amulet safely inside a little sack. They all agreed and set off to where the unicorns were waiting for them.'

'Well, how did it all end?' asked a sleepy little pixie. The fire crackled and glowed, giving off weird shadows that flickered and danced in the night. All the other pixies and elves huddled a little closer round it.

The elf, continued his story, a little annoyed at being interrupted. 'The moonqueen was so pleased when they all returned safely with the magic amulet. She immediately restored the dragon's fire breathing powers and all the fairy folk were rewarded. A large party was organised and everyone in the Enchanted Wood came to dance and everything ended so happily. 'Did you like that story?' asked the elf bursting with pride.

'Ooooh yes,' said all the fairy folk excitedly.

'I have a story to tell, would you like to hear it?' said a pixie.

'It is getting late,' said another pixie stifling a yawn, 'but I suppose we can hear one more, before we go to bed.'

All the others agreed with squeaks of joy and threw some more wood on the fire. The pixie cleared his throat and began his tale. 'One day in the Enchanted Wood ...'

CHARLIE THE GUINEA PIG'S BIG ADVENTURE
Mimie

It was summer and Charlie the ginger guinea pig opened his eyes early in the morning to find the sun already shining through the big garage windows and into his cage. Charlie stretched and yawned in the warm sunshine. 'Morning Pickles,' he said to his friend who shared his cage with him. 'Wake up, it's a beautiful day and I feel like going on an adventure!'

'Oh no,' replied Pickles sleepily, 'not another one of your ideas.' He snuggled down again into his bed of hay and waited for the lady they called Mum to bring them their breakfast.

Sugar and Treacle, two little girl guinea pigs were waking up in the cage next door and were chatting to each other in little squeaky voices while Smokey, the grey rabbit, and his girlfriend Betsey, were banging their feet on the floors of their hutches.

Presently, Mum came into the garage to give them all their breakfasts and she always sang them a jolly little song to wake them all up which went like this: *'Hello Smokey, hello Betsey, hello little guinea pigs, hello little children'*, and Charlie always did a little dance in his hutch while she sang. Then Mum fed them lovely things, filled their water bottles and put them in their runs for the day.

'We are so lucky,' said Smokey, 'to live in this lovely place with our friends, with loads to eat and a kind mum to love us.'

'Yes, I know that,' said Charlie, 'but I still feel like going on an adventure - is anyone going to come with me?'

They all shook their heads and carried on playing, chasing each other round their runs, running through tunnels, throwing plastic flowerpots about and eating.

'Oh well,' said Charlie, 'I will just have to go on my own.' He managed to dig a hole under the wire of his run and out into the garden. He was free in the big world! 'See you later,' said Charlie and scampered off, through the gate at the end of the garden and into the woods beyond.

Charlie felt very happy and whistled a little tune as he walked along. 'Good morning Charlie,' said the squirrels who were playing 'chase' up and down the trees, 'be careful you don't get lost; the woods are very big and there are lots of things around that could hurt you.'

'I won't get lost,' said Charlie, laughing, and carried on walking. There were lots of things to play with in the woods, stones to roll about and twigs to chew. Suddenly, he came to a door set into a bank of earth and Charlie thought he would see who lived there, so he banged on the door with the red door knocker and shouted through the letter box, 'Hello, I'm Charlie, it's a lovely day, will you come out and play with me?'

'Go away,' boomed a loud voice, 'I'm Mr Badger and I only come out when it's dark, you have woken me up.'

'Sorry,' said Charlie and hurried away.

Next, he came to a family of rabbits playing outside their burrow. 'Hi Charlie,' they said, 'want to play with us? We are playing hide-and-seek.'

'Yes please,' replied Charlie and ran off to hide and the rabbits had to find him, but as he was such a bright ginger colour they found him very quickly! Mum rabbit came out of her burrow and brought them all carrot sandwiches for lunch. Then Charlie waved goodbye and went on his way. 'This is great,' said Charlie out loud. 'I love being free to do as I like.'

He came to a clearing in the woods where some birds were holding a singing contest. 'Hello Charlie,' they chirped, 'want to see if you can sing?' So Charlie joined in and all the birds clapped and cheered him and flew about while Charlie sang.

'I enjoyed that,' said Charlie as he waved goodbye.

Suddenly, Charlie realised that it was getting a bit colder and darker and he didn't really know where he was and he started to feel a little afraid. 'I must get home,' he said, 'but which way do I go?' By now, he was getting tired and his tiny legs began to ache and then, to make things worse, a cat jumped out at him from behind a bush because he thought Charlie was a big mouse. Charlie ran as fast as he could and managed to hide under some leaves so that the cat couldn't find him. Now it was really dark and Charlie was hungry and frightened. He kept walking and came upon a family of foxes and, as Charlie wasn't sure if they would be friendly, he hid behind a tree until they went by. 'What can I do?' cried Charlie. 'I'm never going to find my way home.' Then, just when he'd started to get really frightened, he came upon Mr Badger's house and Mr Badger was just coming out of his front door, wrapping a warm scarf round his neck. 'Oh, Mr Badger, please help me,' said Charlie, 'I am so tired and I'm lost.'

'Don't worry,' replied Mr Badger, 'jump on my back and I'll take you back home.'

'Thank you, thank you,' said Charlie and quickly climbed on to Mr Badger's back.

As Mr Badger lumbered through the woods with Charlie clinging to his back, they could see a torch shining in the distance and could hear Mum's voice calling and calling because, of course, when she had come to put them all in their hutches for the night and give them their tea, she had found that Charlie was missing and had been out in the woods for hours looking for him. 'Don't worry,' Mr Badger shouted, 'I have him safe,' and to Charlie's delight, the little gate leading into his garden came into view and there was Mum running towards him.

'Thank you so much Mr Badger,' she said, gathering Charlie up in her arms. 'I thought I had lost him and I was so unhappy.' Charlie snuggled up close to her and soon he was safe, back in his cage with Pickles and all his friends round him in the warmth of the garage with a lovely plateful of food to eat.

As his Mum turned out the light and all the little friends settled down to sleep, Charlie murmured, 'I enjoyed my adventure but I'll never leave my home again because everything I want is here,' and he curled up in his bed of hay with Pickles and went happily to sleep.

THE NEW WEAPON
Jillian A Nagra

Like all little boys, Justin was mischievous, loved playing practical jokes on family and friends, was crazy over football and cricket and was even captain of his school's football team. But most of all - he loved listening to the stories his grandfather related, of those heroes of Shikar, like Jim Corbet. And if the truth be known, secretly he yearned to be a hunter and bag trophies to place upon his mantel, much like the Shikars of yonder years. 'Phooey!' he said to those environmentalists and animal conservationists. 'Animals are meant to be hunted,' said he. 'We are superior beings and we have the power over their lives ...'

Now the big day dawned - his 12th birthday, and he jumped out of bed in anticipation, showered and hurriedly dressed, pulling on his favourite pair of faded and tattered jeans and a bright red T-shirt (which reflected his joyous mood ...) since it was Saturday there was no school to attend. Justin was full of excitement and slid down the banisters where his family awaited him.

'Happy birthday, darling,' Mom said and placed a big kiss on his forehead.

'Yiech! Mom, I'm too old to be kissed,' he complained, but was nonetheless happy. His six-year-old sister, Sarah, bounded up to him, gave him a big hug and a little box, which he hastily tore open, not even bothering to read the card enclosed. 'Wow!' Justin exclaimed. 'A chronograph watch, thanks Sarah.'

'It's from Mama and me,' chirped Sarah.

Next, his grandparents and father came forward.

'Happy birthday, boy, hope you are going to be more responsible now that you are almost a man,' boomed his father and with his words, gave him a tight squeeze.

Grandpa was standing slightly behind Grandma and in his hand was a long box. Now, although Justin wanted to rush to his grandpa and tear open the present, good manners prevailed and he waited, although rather impatiently I may add, till such time, it was given to him. Which was all of ten seconds!

'God bless, darling Jus,' said his grandma in her sweet voice that Jus loved so much to hear, for her voice reminded him of the tinkling brook that he usually went and sat by when he felt a little down. She put her hand on his head in blessing, but Justin was now busy looking beyond and at his grandpa's hands and the mysterious box they held.

'Come here, boy!' bellowed his grandpa in his booming voice, and once Justin went up to him, Grandpa placed the box in his arms. 'Now take care,' cautioned his grandpa, 'don't hurt yourself.'

But Justin was barely listening to his grandpa's words. His barely, contained excitement did not permit reasonable thought just now. He sat down at the breakfast table and gingerly unwrapped the present. 'Yippee!' Justin whooped. 'Thank you Grandpa ... thank you ... I simply love my present and I love you.' Forgetting what a big 12-year-old boy he was for a brief moment, he threw himself into his grandpa's arms and kissed him all over his stubbly chin.

Can you guess what the mysterious box contained? No prizes for guessing, mind you! Well, I won't keep you in suspense any longer.

It was a beautiful rifle, all gleaming metal and polished wood, enclosed in a beautiful box lined with velvet and inscribed, 'To my little Shikar, with love on your 12th birthday', signed 'Grandpa'. He thought he would burst with happiness, he was so excited and in such a hurry to run out of the house with his rifle and ammunition, that he didn't notice the hurt in his father's eyes. You see, Justin, in his haste to run outdoors, had failed to notice another box lying beautifully packed and placed on his side of the table. His mother, noticing what had happened, tried to soften the blow and said, 'You can give it to him when he returns from his 'hunt', which won't be too long I suspect,' and with that she went about her chores in preparation for tonight's party in Justin's honour.

Justin, on the other hand, was the happiest boy in the world right now, and he whistled as he traipsed along in the woods which were fairly close to his house, thinking, *I've just got to bag my first trophy today.* So determined was he on his quest that he failed to notice the beauty surrounding him.

The flowers were in full bloom, hordes of beautifully plumed birds were resplendent in their colourful glory. The trees loomed majestically, towering above, the branches of most straining with the heavily laden fruit and berries upon their boughs, and up ahead, on one particular tree, upon its branch sat a bushy-tailed grey squirrel, an acorn in its tiny paws, busily gnawing at it hungrily. Justin saw the squirrel and slowly brought the rifle to his shoulder so as not to scare the tiny animal. He adjusted the rifle's sight on his game and prepared to shoot ...

But alas! He couldn't. The little squirrel dropped the acorn it was clutching and clambered nearer to where Justin was standing and peered at him inquisitively with those beautiful, gentle eyes. Justin's heart melted, he dropped his rifle and extended his hand to the little creature who, unafraid, jumped onto his arm. For a moment or two, Justin was too afraid to even breathe, or so it seemed, for fear of sending the little creature scuttling away. He just stood there transfixed, as if rooted to the spot, and thought, *how can I shoot such a beautiful little creature?* He was soon roused from his reverie when he felt the squirrel pounce onto his head and back to his home in the tree and out of sight. Justin apprehensively picked up the now offensive rifle from where it lay on the grass and made his way home ...

'Hi, son,' greeted his father as Justin came up the garden path, 'done any hunting?'

'No Dad ... there ... was this squirrel, but I just could not bring myself to kill it,' Justin looked ashamed.

His father rose out of his chair and handed Justin the present that had gone unnoticed earlier that day. 'Here, son,' said his father. 'I'm proud of you.'

'But Dad...' Justin tried to explain that he had not 'bagged' his trophy, you see he thought his father had misunderstood him.

But his father was not listening and, instead, placed the package in Justin's hands. 'Open it Jus, I think you'll like what I've got for you.'

And what nestled within its folds of tissue paper was a brand new Yashika camera, zoom lens, flash and all. Justin was momentarily stunned and overwhelmed at the same time. 'Hey, now I can bag as many trophies as I want and not hurt any living, beautiful creature!' exclaimed Justin.

Little did he notice the smug look on his mother's face. She in fact knew her gentle son was incapable of hurting anyone's feelings, let alone taking a life. But Justin was too busy inspecting his brand new weapon to notice his mother, or anyone else for that matter. He was totally occupied 'loading' the camera with film and thinking, *I hope that little squirrel will be there tomorrow* ...

JESSICA'S MAGIC UMBRELLA
Doris Dowling

One grey, gloomy afternoon, Jessica went to the shops with her mother. They walked there because it wasn't too far. When they reached the shopping centre it started to rain - cold, drizzly rain, and Jessica began to feel rather miserable.

They stopped to look in the window of a shop that sold umbrellas and although Jessica was wearing her nice red anorak and shiny blue wellingtons, her mother said that she would buy her an umbrella to cheer her up.

Inside the shop there were all kinds of umbrellas. Some were big, black and important-looking, some were covered with pretty flowers, and there were others in all the colours of the rainbow. They all looked too big for Jessica, who was only a little girl. Then she saw a small one that was just right. It had a bright red handle that curved at the end, so that if she wanted to she could hang it on her arm. When it was opened up, it was like the sunshine - red and bright yellow - and it had two big, merry eyes and a wide smiley mouth.

On the way home there was a little breeze and suddenly, the umbrella gave a tug and, with Jessica still holding on tightly, flew high into the air. They flew above the supermarket, above the houses and higher still, above the church steeple. The weathercock at the top of the steeple was so surprised that he turned round and round for several minutes and people on the ground couldn't tell which way the wind was blowing.

Over fields and hedgerows and across a wide silver river they flew. Then, a small wind caught up with them and, puffing out its cheeks, blew them towards the sea. Its brothers and sisters joined in the fun and playfully huffed and puffed them this way and that.

'Oh please stop it!' cried Jessica.

Her umbrella shook itself at the mischievous winds and they fled.

'Hi!' screamed a seagull as he nearly bumped into Jessica. 'Look where you are going!' He was cross because he had dropped a fish that he had just caught for his tea.

A little aeroplane dived down to have a closer look. 'Well really,' he said, 'birds, jet planes, helicopters - and now little girls with umbrellas. Whatever next? Soon there will be no room in the sky for little aeroplanes like me.'

'Don't take any notice of him,' chirped a passing swallow, 'he's always moaning and droning. I'm on my way to Africa for the winter. See you next year. Happy landings!'

Jessica laughed as something tickled her cheek. It was a small, fluffy white cloud. It stayed for a while, then floated off into the blue sky.

Soon, she was sitting on a golden, sandy beach, her new umbrella protecting her from the hot sun. There were more umbrellas at the other end of the beach with people sitting underneath them. They were brightly coloured and much, much bigger than hers. *But I shouldn't think they are as clever as mine,* she thought.

'Hello, what are you doing here?' asked a large crab. He walked sideways all around her and admired himself in her shiny wellingtons.

After a while, Jessica heaped up some of the sand with her hands and made a lovely sandcastle, then decorated it with shells. Just as she was putting a lovely big shell right on the top, she looked down and saw that the sea had crept closer, and her boots were getting very wet.

By now, Jessica was feeling rather hot and thirsty and besides, it was time for tea. 'I think I would like to go home now, please,' she said, picking up her umbrella.

The umbrella tugged at her hand and before you could say, 'My goodness, what an adventure!' she found herself once more with her mother. It had stopped raining, the sun was shining and her new umbrella was quite dry.

'Why are your boots so wet?' her mother asked.

But Jessica only smiled a secret smile as she carefully folded her magic umbrella.

PETER AND THE FOREST
Janet Middleton

The daylight began to fade. Peter's dad lit the campfire. His mum began supper on the camp stove. The forest round the clearing filled with scuffling, rustling leaves.

Peter went to investigate. *I won't go far,* Peter thought to himself. *Maybe I'll see some badgers, or a fox.* Then Peter felt prickles on the back of his neck rise. A cold shiver went down his spine. Something ran across his shoe. Giving himself a shake, whatever it was went scurrying up a tree. The moon eerily peeked through the tree branches ...

This is scary, very scary! Two eyes looked down from the tree, big and yellow, *tu-whit, tu-whoo!* Oh! Peter took a deep breath - an owl. He picked up a big stick. 'I'll whop, hit, anything that comes near me.'

Further along the path, more noises. A fox ran into the undergrowth. 'Wow, he's a big one,' Peter said to himself. But this part of the forest was thicker. Peter felt cold and hungry and wondered, *how do I get back to camp? Oh, I wish I'd never left the camp.*

Peter's nerves jumped about inside him. 'Mum, Mum, Mum!' he cried. *The camp, it must be around this bush, or that tree. Where's the path gone? I'm hungry, I only wanted to explore, not get lost.* Then he heard a rough voice coming from behind a huge tree. He listened ...

'If we're quiet, we'll catch them badgers and get a good price for them.'

Peter felt his prickles rise at the back of his neck. Keeping silent, he peeked round the tree trunk. Two big, burly men stood there with nets, waiting on the badgers coming back.

Oh no, you're not going to catch those badgers if I can help it! Peter to the rescue! His dad had said about badgers needing protection. Peter, hunger forgotten and scared out of his wits, realised the badgers couldn't defend themselves, but he could do it for them! As the men approached the sett, Peter's heart thumped. His mouth went dry as he crept up behind the men.

Peter saw the badgers going into their sett; the two men didn't know he was there. Peter tapped his pocket. *Of course! My cub whistle. I'd forgotten I'd brought it.* First Peter went in and under the thicket, making as much noise as he could, thumping the branches with his stick, then blowing his whistle as loud as he could. One of the men spotted Peter and grabbed him by the collar.

'You young git, you've spoiled our night's work,' he growled.

A fox barked, Peter trembled, the forest creatures put up such a noise! Then lights flashed. The forest lit up and voices boomed. 'Halt right there!' a forest ranger shouted through a megaphone. The policemen grabbed the running men.

'I've got them, Sergeant.'

'You'll be carted off in the van to the local jail. In the morning you'll be in court; our magistrate is very down on poachers. Good on you, young fellow.'

Just at that point, Peter's dad appeared. 'There you are Peter, we've been looking for you for ages.'

'You should be proud of him,' said the ranger, 'if it hadn't been for your son's cub whistle, we wouldn't have caught them poachers we've been after for ages.'

Peter was still a bit shaken, but glad the badgers were safe. At eight years old, it had been quite an adventure.

THE OLDEST CHRISTMAS PRESENT
Pamela Harvey

Doreen the Dinosaur wandered through the tall ferns. She ate some of them. They did not give her indigestion, but they would be poisonous to humans. In these days of long ago, there were no humans. Or were there? Doreen had heard stories of strange little creatures. She was only little too, and she wondered if she could walk the long distance to where these creatures lived. And what was a human? They were said to be very clever. Doreen tossed her head, and her long neck quivered in annoyance. They could not be anything like as clever as dinosaurs. *They* had been around for millions of years.

She trailed her way through the ferns, looking up at the towering trees that were called cycads. Doreen was a brontosaurus. Some people call them 'apatosaurus'. She had a friend, Steggia Saurus. (Stegosaurus - a different kind of dinosaur.)

They were both friendly with a triceratops called Tricon. He scoffed at the idea of there being anyone as clever as dinosaurs. 'Humans!' he'd say. 'They don't exist. No one has seen them.'

Suddenly Doreen saw her two friends eating some of the green leaves near the bottom of a tall cycad.

'Hi!' they shouted.

She answered quietly. She wanted to look for humans. She knew they would both scoff at her if she told them.

'Where are you goin'?' Tricon saw her expression and wondered if she was up to something. Mischief perhaps?

'Nowhere. Just walking.'

'Looks like somewhere to me. You've something on your mind. We'll come along with you.' He looked at Steggia who was munching a large mouthful of green leaves. Slowly, but she enjoyed her food.

'I'm getting something for Mother,' said Doreen. She noted their curious glances, she was not going to tell them she was looking for humans.

'We'll still come along with you,' Tricon knew she was hiding the truth. He smiled.

'No - I'll see you both later. I'm in a rush.'

'Right - no problem,' Steggia went on eating.

Tricon made to follow Doreen.

'Get lost,' she told him angrily.

'What if you meet a T-rex?'

'I'll deal with him!'

Tricon laughed and laughed. 'You - a baby like you?'

Doreen drew herself up with dignity. 'Yes - me. My mother nearly killed one the other day. She gave him such a whack with her tail. And she was fighting to protect me, too. But old Tyrannosaurus - he just slunk away - he couldn't cope.'

'OK, suit yourself, but don't blame me if the next time I see you you're in little pieces. Or just crumbs.'

Doreen left them then. She wandered on and on, until it began to get dark. The tallest trees hid the moon, though it peeped out quite often, and when the clouds parted she saw the twinkling stars.

Suddenly a shape loomed up ahead of her. It was above her on a hillside. It was a small, sturdy shape. She got nearer. She could make out the face. It was square-jawed and wide. Coarse hair hung over a low forehead. Then, in the moonlight she could see the creature was smiling. Then it grunted.

'Ug-Og,' it said, pointing to itself.

'It's a human,' whispered Doreen to herself.

'Ug-Og,' repeated the creature. It nodded toward Doreen.

'Dor-een,' said Doreen slowly. *Dinosaurs have much prettier names,* she thought. She was not prepared for the reply.

'Ug-Og pretty, too.'

He could read her thoughts. She had never heard of humans doing that. Well, he must be special. Doreen realised suddenly that she was lost. Then, the boy took her arm. She noticed the long red-brown hairs on his arm, but he smiled at her in a very friendly way. They walked along together. Soon they came to where the trees and ferns thinned a little. Doreen did not know the place. Above them, not far away, on the hill, was a large rock. The boy climbed onto it. He held out his hand to Doreen. He pulled her up beside him. She was only a very little dinosaur.

He said one word, tapping the stone, 'Magic.'

Doreen repeated it. 'Magic?'

'This stone can fly. I just tell it to.'

Then there came a roar from the forest, not very far away.

Doreen froze. 'T-rex! Oh no!' She knew how fast they could run, and this one sounded hungry. 'Ready for a snack, or two ...' her words were scared.

The roar sounded again. Bellowing, the tyrannosaurus burst into the clearing. He opened his big mouth, his teeth shone in the moonlight. Then he jumped...

Suddenly Doreen was aware of a big jolt. She saw the T-rex near, smelt his breath. Then, she felt the lifting ...

She heard the boy say something softly to the stone, and then saw what had happened. They were up in the air, the stone carrying them both, flying out of danger, higher, ever higher until they left the T-rex behind, growling as his meal was snatched from him at the last moment. As they left the tallest cycad trees behind, they saw the moon clear and the stars brilliant above them. They almost felt they were among them. Above the cloud cover they raced, on and on.

As they swiftly flew, the sky gradually turned from black to deepest blue, then to lighter blue, then to the shimmering beauty of dawn. Doreen looked down. Ug-Og held her firmly on one side. She saw below them square shapes and a straight track. She saw more humans, wearing clothes - peculiar drapy things - round them. Some wore metallic skirts. The stone was going down, going to land. Ug-Og whispered magic words to guide it. They landed on a green hillside. Strange woolly animals were standing there eating the green stuff. Some were wandering onto the track where the people were. The ones wearing metal skirts and helmets were shouting at some other people. Doreen and Ug-Og did not know what they were saying, but the people shouted at looked both angry and a bit scared.

'Romans!' Ug-Og said to Doreen. 'The future,' he added.

That's why I met him, thought Doreen, *he is of the future too, but not so far as these people.*

The Romans turned in disbelief at the sight of Doreen and Ug-Og landing on the stone. Meanwhile, the sheep baa-ed and got in the way of the other people, who shouted at them too.

Then another strange animal appeared on the scene. He looked straight at Doreen and her friend. She saw they were meant to follow him. The Romans were intent on clearing the highway. A shepherd prodded the sheep gently in another direction. He too looked at Doreen and Ug-Og, as if he recognised the boy. He did look startled at Doreen's appearance, but he said nothing. Another shepherd nudged him and pointed to the east.

The Romans finally got around to Doreen. 'What are you doing here?' one of them called out.

Another smiled. 'Cornelius, it's a dragon - but just a baby. I never thought they really existed. Oh well - leave the poor little thing alone, and the child. We've enough to deal with.'

The sheep were still milling around, blocking the highway. Cornelius swore in Latin, but smiled and threw up his hands.

The strange creature came closer to Doreen and brayed, then trotted off, nodding to her and the boy to follow.

Then another Roman shouted at them and tried to grab Doreen. He slipped, but picked up the boy. But Doreen was so quick.

'Ouch!' Ug-Og was taken by surprise as he felt something around his waist. Doreen had hooked her tail around him, dragging him a few yards and then lashing out at the Roman. They all saw her scales glisten in the early morning sunlight. She was little, but powerful - to them. They stood at a safe distance. She heard the words 'Dragon!' and 'Let them go. See, they are following the donkey'.

The donkey trotted along until he came to a doorway in a wall. He looked back at Doreen and Ug-Og, then led the way down some steps.

'It's a cave,' whispered Doreen, 'I live in a cave.'

There were a couple of animals there, and three people. Two of them were grown-up, but one was only tiny.

Once inside the stable-cave, Doreen felt less frightened. Escape. She looked at the humans and they looked at her and smiled. They were not afraid of her. She felt they thought she was cute. Then the little one smiled too. She sensed it was especially for her. He held out a little hand. Doreen suddenly wished she had something to give this baby, some present, so that they would never really ever be quite apart again.

Then Ug-Og flicked something off her back. It was a piece of prehistoric fern that had come with them on the magic stone. Mischievously he had put it there at the start of the trip. On the journey through time, it had flowered.

Ug-Og laughed. 'From us - to you,' he said.

Doreen gave it to the little one. He took the flower and held it against his cheek.

Ug-Og smiled broadly. Doreen felt so happy. This was a very special baby. She was so glad she had brought him the oldest Christmas present. The oldest in the world, but it came with love.

THE RAINBOW TEAPOT
Emma Lockyer

There once was a witch, whose name was Hildee. Hildee was a good witch who loved making spells and potions from the various herbs and flowers in her garden. Hildee lived in a huge forest, in a tiny thatched cottage with lots of flowers growing in the front garden.

It was a fine summer's day when Hildee decided to make a cup of tea from the new teapot she had just bought at the local flea market. The teapot had cost twenty pence and Hildee thought it was a bargain, just right for two cups of tea. The only thing was, the teapot was an odd colour of brown, the colour of mud really, but Hildee saw past the colour and knew how useful it would be. Anyway, perhaps she could magic up a tea cosy (Hildee was no good at knitting).

Just as Hildee put the kettle on over her fire, there was a gentle thud of a letter coming through the door. Hildee went to fetch it. There on the floor was a pink envelope. Hildee opened it up eagerly, an invitation to a sixties' night at the Cauldron Club! Hildee had been a member for years; she'd joined when she was a lot younger, with her best friend Edith. *'Oooh,* I must tell Edith!' Hildee rushed to the telephone and dialled Edith's number. 'Edith? Are you going to the sixties' night at the Cauldron Club?'

There was an excited cackle from the other end of the phone.

'Have you got anything in the way of stuff for hair? I don't even have a bottle of shampoo!'

There was silence from the other end.

'Edith, you have got to help me, you know my hair hasn't been combed for years, let alone washed, can you come over? I'll do yours! Then you can help me magic up something, like a hairstyle?'

'Of course I will come over. Put the kettle on, I'll be there in a jiffy.'

Edith and Hildee pored over the old spell book that Hildee got from the top shelf in the kitchen. The book was so old some of the ingredients had changed names, so between the two of them, they managed to remember what things used to be called in the olden days, but not quite.

'It says here lavender and lilac, bushtail and silack? What are bushtail and silack, Hildee?'

'Dooh, just put in the lavender and lilac.'

Edith put in twice the amount of lavender and lilac to make up for the lack of bushtail and silack. 'Then it says ...' Edith's long, scrawny finger ran through the word, but there was no recognition in her face at all.

'Give it here!' Hildee took the glasses off Edith's face and put them on herself. 'Devil's throat and gossamer leaves, Delilah's 'kerchief, and a dash of summer wine. There! I think I know what it requires.' Hildee went to her cupboard of the usual ingredients and got out a bottle of blackberry wine she was saving for winter, some sweets left over from Hallowe'en, and some chocolate leaves. Hildee then pulled out the handkerchief from the sleeve in her cardigan and popped them all in her cauldron. It began to boil immediately and exploded in Hildee's face! Edith cackled, and handed Hildee her handkerchief.

'Well, while that's fixing, we will have a cup of tea.' Hildee went to get the teapot, but did not notice that the teapot now had a purple spot on it, sliding down to the bottom.

'I say, Hildee, that teapot's a bit of a disaster!'

'Never you mind Edith, it was a bargain and it's useful!' Hildee poured in the hot water. 'Do you like blackberry tea?'

'Don't you have any blueberry?'

'Erm ... no.'

Edith was crestfallen, she would have liked blueberry, she liked blueberries. 'Oh well, I'll have blackberry then,' sounding disappointed.

As Edith lifted the cup to her long, pointed noise, she could smell something familiar. She sniffed and sniffed again. Hildee had already taken a mouthful of her favourite tea, and was enjoying her refreshment. Edith took a mouthful of her tea and realised that Hildee had indeed made her a cup of blueberry tea! 'How nice of you Hildee, you had blueberry tea after all!'

Hildee looked at Edith, replacing her cup. She could smell blueberries and followed the smell to Edith's cup. Hildee smelt her own cup. Hildee then went over to the teapot. There was a purple stripe all the way down on one side, and when she lifted the lid, there was only hot water inside, no tea at all! Hildee knew she had put tea leaves in there, but they were nowhere to be seen! 'Hmm. You are right, Edith, that is blueberry tea! And I have blackberry tea! Enjoy!'

As the spell-making progressed, the teapot got splashed again and again. Hildee kept making cups of tea, and asked Edith if she would like to try another flavour. Edith tried various types of different teas, after all Hildee did make blueberry tea, but she only needed to put one type of tea in the teapot, and out would come the flavour of tea Edith had requested.

Eventually the cauldron was ready. Edith and Hildee washed their hair in the mixture. It was all sticky and smelled like a hair salon, it even stuck to Edith's fingernails. Hildee had to use her feet to get her hands out of Edith's hair, because the mixture set like concrete! At last their hair was up, Hildee and Edith had beehives, which made them a good foot taller. Hildee cast a magic spell and the beehives became balls of ice cream, in various different shades. The teapot had so many different stripes and spots from the mixture Hildee was in too much of a hurry to wash it all off.

Hildee and Edith got on their broomsticks and sped off to the Cauldron Club. There were many different hairstyles, Edith noticed, but at least no one looked like herself or Hildee, they were wearing stripes of different colours because Hildee had not washed her hands. After the spell, everything Hildee touched became a rainbow! Even Edith's fingernails were rainbows, and now she was looking at Hildee's feet, yes, rainbow toenails! Hildee rushed into the ladies and washed her hands, too late now to reverse the spell, besides her hair looked too good to reverse. Anyway, the spell would run out at midnight, just before the winner would be called! Edith and Hildee had the time of their lives at the sixties night; all of the old music made memories of their youth come flooding back. Then the announcement came:

'This evening we have had strong competition for the best dressed witch and wizard from the sixties, so we have decided to add an additional prize for the most inventive costume. Tonight that honour, with a prize of lunch with that wizard of the garden, Alan Saltmarsh, goes to Edith and Hildee!'

Edith and Hildee were jumping up and down screaming, they had never won anything before, but before they could think of what day to have lunch, there was a loud high-pitched tone coming from the microphone. Alan Saltmarsh had taken hold of the microphone and was looking down at the two witches in the audience.

'I would like to have a dance with young Hildee here, but that would not be fair to her friend, so I have asked for that new boy on the block, all the way from Ireland, to assist me! Ladies and gentlemen, I present to you Dermot, the green-fingered leprechaun!'

Edith clapped her hands. In came Dermot with a full head of brown hair, something she could get her long scrawny fingers into, practising for her hairdressing! They all arranged to have their lunch at the Stone Cold Priory, a favourite eating place for witches.

Hildee put the hot water in the teapot, and replaced the lid. The lid was now a rainbow of colours, as was the rest of the teapot. Hildee no longer had to put tea leaves in the teapot to get a refreshing brew. All she had to do was say which tea she would like to have, put in the hot water, and there would be the cup of tea of her dreams. Hildee decided not to magic up a tea cosy, she liked the colour of her new teapot because it reminded her of the sixties' night competition she had won with Edith, and of the wonderful time she had with Alan Saltmarsh.

Alan had been a most pleasant chap; he helped her design paths through her flowers, so that she could pick and water them. He also introduced flowering lollipop trees, a liquorice bush and chocolate cocoa, and vanilla-dusted bonbon flowers in the patch under the trees.

Edith went on to win an award for Dermot's hair, before he went back to Ireland, but they still keep in touch.

THE FOX AND THE CURSE
Susan Roffey

John and Susan peered wistfully out of misty windows; snow covered every tree and plant. *Soon, the stone cat will be covered, lost to an ocean of whiteness,* Susan thought, *like a castle built of sand, slowly lost beneath oncoming waves.* Christmas holidays were not much fun without Dad.

'Mum,' John said, 'when Dad is home again, can we all go on holiday together?'

'Of course. Daddy misses us as well. He said in his letter that you will have a wonderful time at his auntie Mauds, she has a great house to explore. Ned is her helper. Daddy said he must be ancient; he was old when he was a boy.'

'Read Dad's letter again, please Mum.'

'Once more, then we must pack.'

The humming of the train seemed hypnotic, their eyes slowly closed. Susan curled up to Mum, put her thumb in her mouth and soon fell fast asleep. Mummy smiled at John. Susan was only six; John was ten, a very grown-up ten she thought.

'I'm cold, Mummy,' Susan said as she huddled up close to Mum.

They were waiting on a cold, dark station. Ned was picking them up, he was very late. Aunt Maud didn't have a telephone, so they just had to wait.

A clip-clopping sound made John turn. 'Look! It's a horse and carriage.'

'Oh, isn't it grand,' said Susan.

'Hello,' Ned said, 'Mrs White?'

'Yes.'

'Scramble in, there are warm blankets inside. Sorry I'm late, the lane was blocked with snow. I had to clear a path through.'

Soon they were sitting by a roaring fire, under cosy candlelight, tucking into crumpets with home-made jam and hot, steamy mugs of creamy milk.

'It's lovely to have you stay, I don't get many visitors,' said Aunt Maud.

The house was huge, as it was dark the children couldn't see much.

'Come on now, time for bed. There's lots to explore in the morning.'

Sleep came quickly.

'John, look out the window.'

'Oh Sue, it's cold out there.'

'No, the snow is almost gone, it's raining. Look at the garden.'

Grudgingly, John climbed out of bed. 'It's huge.'

'There are woods and a lake. Are those mountains John?'

'Look, there's a heron, Susan, it's in my bird book. Let's go and tell Mum.'

'Breakfast first,' insisted Mum, as Susan chatted eagerly.

They tucked into large bowls of porridge.

'Now off you go, be good.'

'Yes Mum,' they chorused.

The house was a castle with towers, the battlements mostly broken down now. Susan said the ceilings were as high as the sky. Paintings hung on many walls, shiny suits of armour lined the entrance hall, a great spiral staircase seemed to go on forever, carvings and statues were everywhere and great tapestries adorned the walls.

The children wandered around the rooms gently touching the furniture; black oak pieces too large for John to reach the surfaces. They ran from room to room; much was covered in white sheets. They lost all track of time and had reached the third floor when a gong sounded. Susan nearly jumped out of her skin.

'It's time for dinner,' John said.

'How do you know, John?'

He remembered his dad's letter. 'Auntie bangs a gong when it's time to eat. Besides, I am hungry.'

'Me too,' she said.

It was their favourite: sausages and mash, with peaches and custard to follow.

'How are you doing with your exploring?'

'I love the paintings. Are they all our ancestors?'

'Yes, John.'

'Some people look a little like Daddy. The painting in the great hall, Aunt Maud, sometimes I think I see a fox and when I look again, it's gone.'

'It is a painting of this house when it was first built in the 15th century. There's an old book in the library, it tells a tale of a spell cast over the house. There was a fire many years ago, the book was damaged. The only words left are part of a clue, but they don't make sense.'

'What are they?' John asked.

'Oh, I am a bit muddled in my memory, dear, we'll find the book another day.'

Susan had curled up on Mummy's lap, listening to a story about Peter Rabbit.

'Come help me do this puzzle, John, there's another day to explore tomorrow.'

It was cosy by the fire listening to the rain and wind battering at the old windows. Aunt Maud told John lots about the people in the paintings.

While eating breakfast the next day, Aunt Maud placed a box on the table. 'Open this,' she said, 'and find the place it belongs.'

'What is it?' Susan cried.

John felt all round the box for the catch.

'Let me look,' Susan said. As she reached for it, her finger released its catch and the lid flew open. 'It's magic!' Out fell a key, a great black shiny cat was at its head. 'It's a witch's key!' Susan cried.

'Don't be daft, there's no such thing as witches.'

'Yes, in my comic about Gobbelino, the witch's cat ...'

'It's only a story.' John was ten after all, he didn't believe in such things.

The children searched in every place a key would fit, but to no avail.

'John, I'm tired, can we have a rest?'

'All right, it's nearly time for tea.'

Tucking the children up in bed that night, Mummy suggested they should play outside tomorrow.

'Race you to the lake, Susan.'

'That's not fair, I've got the bread for the ducks.'

John was too far ahead to hear her. She was about to scold him when she saw he was pointing at something.

'The smoke,' John whispered, 'the smoke.'

'What about it?' Susan was getting cross.

'How many fires are alight in the house?'

'Only one, John, Aunt Maud says it's a waste to heat the whole house when one is enough to keep a body warm,' mimicking Aunt Maud. It was quite easy to do, she was lovely but so funny at times.

'Yes,' John said, 'but there are two chimneys with smoke coming out.'

'Let's ask Ned.'

Throwing the bread to the ducks, they ran to find Ned.

'I've seen it too, can't make head nor tail of it,' he said, and then went off muttering to himself.

A fox suddenly ran across the lawn. Susan loved animals and started to run after it. John knew he had best stay with her. It ran through the woods with the children following, under fences, across a field, then back towards the house. It disappeared down a hole by an old dead tree. The children were puffed out. Susan sat on an old branch against the tree and all of a sudden, she fell back into a large, empty space; it was like a door had opened in the tree. John had seen what had happened and was soon following Susan, too surprised to be frightened. John took out his pocket torch and they followed the underground passage. By John's watch, they had been walking for five minutes.

'My legs hurt, John.'

'That's because it's getting steeper.'

The passage ended at a heavy wooden door. It had a large black knocker, shaped like a cat. Susan gasped, 'It's like the key!'

John felt in his pockets for the key. 'It fits!' he said as he turned it. 'Help me push, Susan.'

Surprisingly, the door opened quite easily; they fell on their knees inside the door.

'Are you hurt?' a voice said. Out of the shadows came a tiny man with pixie ears and a bushy tail.

John opened his mouth to speak.

'Let's not say another word until we've had tea.' He clicked his fingers and all at once a table was set with wonderful things to eat.

'Oh!' Susan said.

After tea, they sat by a cosy fire. 'It's rude to point, Susan,' scolded John. Susan had noticed the man's ears and tail had gone.

'I'm Jude, the midget. Many years ago, I stopped wicked witches from stealing my lord's newborn son. The house was newly built and on the night of the grand ball, Nanny had charge of the child in the tallest tower. She was on the stairs listening to the music while the child slept and witches flew in to carry him away. I was once blessed by fairies and given some magic powers. I cast a spell to stop their flight, guards were summoned and they were put to death. Before they died, a spell was put on me, turning me into a fox always to be hunted, until a child finds the wishing well of fools and says the magic words, *one is silver, one is gold, one is copper, all should hold.*

'What does the riddle mean?' John asked.

'I don't know. I may be shot at any time; foxes are hunted.'

'How can we help?'

'Solve the riddle, I think you can.'

The next moment, they were in front of the house.

'John, have we been dreaming?'

'I don't think so.'

The next morning, John asked Aunt Maud about the book. 'Let's see if we can find it. Mum and Susan are going shopping.' She searched the shelves, dust particles fell like snow in the sun's rays through the giant windows. 'Ah,' she cried, 'here it is!'

It was red leather, edged with gold. Inside the front cover was a map of the house and grounds. Beautiful artwork surrounded the lettering, soft petals lay between delicate pages. Towards the back, a page was torn.

'What is the book about?' he asked.

'It's the story of the house, the people who lived here and all the things that took place through the years - a bit like a diary. It's right from the beginning, when the land belonged to fairies.'

'And did it?' he asked.

'Who knows? Strange things do happen here. When I was a child, I saw little people dancing in a circle, with a great red fox lying watching them. My dad said I had been dreaming, but there was a fairy ring worn in the grass where I had seen them.'

'Is there a well in the grounds?'

'No, John.'

'What does the torn page say?'

'Break the spell for all to be well, bring back the life where the cedar fell, solve the riddle when a child finds ... That's it,' Auntie said. 'I don't know when it was torn out, it has always been that way. There is supposed to be a treasure chest hidden somewhere. Now, if we could find that, we could restore this old house.'

John turned to the back page where a picture of the house stood out. 'It's just like the big picture over the fireplace. Look, Auntie, between the trees - is that a well?'

'I do believe it is, but there isn't one, John. It must have been an idea of the artist to add little features in his paintings.'

John said, 'Is it on the big picture.'

'I can't recall,' she said. 'Run along and have a peek.'

John's heart was racing as he stood looking up at the great painting. 'It's there.' He climbed on a chair to see if there was a name on the well; there wasn't. As he started to climb down, John noticed a signature in the corner.

Auntie came up behind him. 'Oh! That's the painter's name, Isaac Fools.'

'Auntie, the well! Look!'

'You're right,' she said. 'I'll get lunch on. Cheese on toast all right?'

'Lovely,' John said, and off she went.

The answer to the riddle must be in the painting, he thought. Suddenly, the tiny flag on the top of the house caught his eye. Three hands were holding three goblets; one was a golden colour, another silver, the other looked almost orange.

Over lunch, John asked Aunt Maud about the flag.

'Like I said, the land was once the fairies. Lord Peter was out riding one day with his manservant, Jude, when they came across this land. On it was a very large Cedar tree. They heard cries of pain. Amongst the branches was a bag and around it swarmed angry bees. Lord Peter held his servant on his shoulders to cut down the bag. They were badly stung. The story is that wicked witches had captured fairy children and the fairies had been searching for them. Because of their bravery, the fairy king rewarded Lord Peter with enough land to build this house. Jude was bestowed with the gift of magic, the pact was sealed with a toast of berry wine and the promise that his house and lands would stand forever. Lord Peter kept the goblets that the toast was made in.

His hand held the goblet of silver, gold for the fairy king and the copper goblet for Jude. It wasn't until many years later that Lord Peter had a flag made of the three hands holding the three goblets, after his faithful servant vanished.'

'That explains it,' John said.

'What does?' replied Auntie.

John started his story all about the chimney smoke, how they had followed the fox and ending up with the little man, their magical tea and his tale of the curse.

'Oh John, do you think you have solved the mystery after hundreds of years? What do we do now?'

'The goblets, Auntie, do they still exist?'

'Yes,' she said. 'Come with me.' She took him into the room with the big black furniture he could not reach. She opened a hidden drawer and took out two keys, stood on a stool, unlocked one of its cupboards, took out a beautiful carved box and gave John the tiny key. He unlocked it. There in green satin, lay three goblets; gold, silver and copper.

They stood before the painting. John held all three goblets in his hand. 'Here is the well of Isaac Fools. Gold, silver, copper are in my hand, toasted with once upon fairy land, so break the spell of witches old, for now is the story told ...'

A voice came from behind them. 'Thank you, John, I am free. I am to live with the fairies. If you ever need me, you need only think of me. Your heart is pure, your greatest wish will come true, this I promise you.' Then he was gone.

Shouts brought them back to reality. 'John, John,' Mummy came in. 'There's a letter from your dad, he's coming home.'

That was John's greatest wish. His daddy had been on a ship which had been lost.

'Aunt Maud, what is in here?' Susan asked, as a panel by the fireplace lay slightly open. She bent down to look. 'It's a letter.' She asked John to read it.

'It's a riddle,' he said. 'Look to your laurels if you want to find greatest treasures of every kind.'

Auntie and John laughed. 'Here we go again,' they said.

Mum and Susan joined in laughing. Everything was going to be all right now.

GRANNY FRY - HER PROBLEM AND ITS SOLUTION
A R Carter

Granny Fry lived in a little country cottage. It had a small lawn in front with flowers in a border all around it, and at the back of the cottage, Granny Fry grew a few vegetables in neat rows and kept three chickens to provide her with eggs. Everything was neat and tidy, just like Granny Fry herself. *A place for everything and everything in its place,* was her motto.

Inside the cottage it was the same - neat and tidy and all sparkly clean, except for *one* corner in the little sitting room. Try as she might, Granny Fry never seemed to be able to keep it clean and tidy all the time. Why do you think that was? Well, she had a friend. His name was Billy and he was a budgerigar and Billy the budgie was responsible for all the mess. Mind you, it wasn't deliberate, well not always. Billy just couldn't help it. When he ate his seed, he liked to plunge his beak right into the little container, shake his head and see what he came up with. This meant that most of the seed scattered - either onto the floor of his cage or, more likely, through the bars onto Granny Fry's carpet below. Then, when Billy wanted a drink, he would fly to the other side of his cage, plunge his head into the water dish to get a beak full and, consequently, most of it went over the side, once more onto Granny Fry's carpet. Oh dear - Granny Fry wondered what she was going to do about it and gave the matter a lot of thought.

Granny Fry went to the village every Wednesday and every Saturday to do her shopping. All the people knew her and it would take her a long time to finish her shopping trip because everyone would stop and chat with her. They *all* called her Granny. 'Hello Granny', 'Mornin' Granny Fry', 'Yoo hoo - how are you Granny Fry?' No one could remember a time when she was ever called anything else.

One Wednesday, she finished her housework, left everything neat and tidy as usual - even Billy's corner - and set off on her shopping trip. She had got as far as the butcher's shop when she bumped into bossy Mrs Farthingale, who always knew everything about everything - or at least she thought she did. They got chatting about this and that and Granny Fry confided to Mrs Farthingale about the problem she was having with Billy's messy corner.

'Oh - that's easily sorted out,' said Mrs Farthingale in a loud voice. 'All you need is one of those little plastic thingamabobs. You fix them around the bottom of the cage with elastic and all the bits go in there. Then you just take it off carefully, take it outside and empty it into the dustbin, give it a quick wash and put it back on again.' She paused for breath and continued, 'I think they've got some in the post office,' and off she went.

Granny Fry stood outside the butcher's shop and thought about this. It looked as though she was deciding what meat to buy, but really what was on her mind was all the information that Mrs Farthingale had given her. Then, with a nod of her head, she turned around and trotted off to the post office where she explained to Polly, the postmistress, what she was looking for. She kept her fingers crossed as Polly went into the back room to rummage around to see if she could find one. Polly came back with a triumphant smile on her face and a 'Budgerigar Cage Tidy' in her hand. Granny Fry was delighted, paid for it and hurried home with her neat little feet making a tip-tapping sound as she sped along.

Because she was *always* neat and tidy, Granny Fry took off her coat and hat and put them in the cupboard, removed her shoes and put on her slippers, put her shopping basket on the kitchen table and only then did she take her special purchase into the sitting room. 'Look, Billy,' she said brightly, 'I think we may have the solution here. I'll just fix it on and we'll see what you think of it.'

The 'Budgerigar Cage Tidy' looked really good when it was finally in place, and Granny Fry thought how lucky it was that it had some blue flowers on it to match Billy's blue feathers. She cleaned up the seed that had got onto the carpet whilst she had been out shopping and hoped it would be the last time she would have to do *that* job - and it was. Granny Fry was delighted, and on her Saturday morning shopping trip, she called at Mrs Farthingale's house to tell her so.

Now *everything* about Granny Fry's house is neat and tidy, with a place for everything and everything in its place. Neat front lawn with a border all around it. Neat back garden with rows of vegetables and three chickens in a neat little run. Neat and tidy and all sparkly clean inside the cottage too - including Billy the budgie's corner.

Granny Fry was neatly and tidily happy.

SNOWDRIFT
J Millington

When Don and Diana got up that morning for breakfast, there was a coating of snow on the ground. They were soon whooping like savages; a lovely day ahead of them.

Their mother made them eat their breakfast, though they were impatient to get out. Their dad got out their sleds and watched them off. Billy, their dog, wasn't going to be left behind and he ran, barking, after them. There was much laughter.

They knew they were going on the Little Mountain, but called to collect their friend, Roland. They wouldn't go without him. They skimmed along, enjoying the sunshine and the snow. It was the first snow of the winter and it had been snowing all night, which neither they nor their families realised. The first snow was rarely heavy.

As their sleds skimmed along, they laughed and shouted in high glee. When they collected Roland, Diana snuggled their dog, Billy, up to her on her sled. If he went on, he'd be exhausted running behind them. He certainly wasn't going to be left behind.

None of them had any thought of danger, but Don realised his friend, Roland, wasn't following them. He stopped and so did Diana. There wasn't a sign of their friend. They knew they'd have to go back and look for him.

Whiteness was everywhere, with not a dark speck anywhere. They were very worried. Where could he be? Diana remembered the last time she'd seen him, so they continued their search for him in one area. After half an hour there was still no sign of Roland. Diana was nearly in tears. How could they go home without him? Then Don had a bright idea - let Billy search for him. The dog was a good sniffer, so he set Billy to search.

Billy seemed to know what was expected of him and his nose went sniffing over the snow. Then he gave a yelp. Don and Diana went over to him, by which time he was digging frantically. Although they couldn't, at first, see anything, they both joined Billy in digging snow. Then, a hand lifted in the snow hole. Roland was buried in a snowdrift. Soon he was out, mercifully alive and unhurt.

He had fallen into a large hole which was full of snow and snow had fallen all around him and covered him. He could not get out, and if it hadn't have been for Billy, he could have died. As it was, they decided to go home.

Their families were glad to see them, as no one had realised how much snow had fallen in the night and it was very dangerous.

Luckily, Billy had been with them. He was a hero, and got an extra bone for his rescue.

ON SUEFARI
Peter Asher

Poorly Boy was at a loose end with no operations and no one to play with. Those children he knew, were all at school where he was too much at risk, so the people doctors cautioned, to follow. Any minute, they said, his poorly heart might look at the clock and decide it, and Poorly Boy ought to be in hospital - or even elsewhere. They said 'elsewhere' very gravely, whilst looking at Mum and Dad, who'd look at one another and look down.

Poorly Boy always looked up, however, at such moments, as he knew he wasn't going anywhere other than up - for he had so much to do; so much to make right in the garden, the street, the world. So many poorly toys to make smile again. So many children to give imaginations so many people to give heart, if not to heal.

Only today was one of those where the sun keeps its arms folded throughout, and birds mutter more than sing upon. Whilst fluffy, merry clouds can't be bothered, blue skies don't get up, grey skies seem to like it and rain clouds threaten to visit before supper. Poorly Boy knew it depended on him alone what the day would do, for he'd been left to make its mind up for it when others of its family members had been bored in his short lifetime.

But Poorly Boy also knew there was great risk attached to these decisions. Often he'd decided the day's fate would rest indoors with a television set, colouring book, or enjoyable hour spent irritating Mum. Often the day wouldn't take its medicine though - and whilst he was refusing to eat his dinner - it was out playing in the bright sunshine, it was defying his decision to stop indoors.

The palm of Poorly Boy's hand was philosophically contemplating these imponderables, this particular loose end with his chin, just after breakfast. His elbow was gently rocking itself to sleep with arm stood to attention on the window ledge, whilst a chorus of fingers tried to drum their personal opinion to palm and chin, either side of his nose. His eyes looked up, and as always, the sky was awaiting his directions. It was Nurse Nelly who suggested some, suddenly from Mum's hands as she entered the kitchen, sat on the tray Mum was carrying.

'Why don't we go hunt calories in the garden?' she said. 'You know what days are - and if we decide to stop in and I spend it defending your mum against you lot, it'll defy us and be nice and sunny while I'm struggling beside Mum versus you and Little Sheeps in here. Whereas if we get our coats on and go out on a calorie hunting expedition, it'll either join us with a grin on its face, or cry all over us. We'll just have to take our chances.'

Just as Nellie finished, Mum unbeknownst to herself, agreed. 'Why don't you put your coat on and go outside and risk it? It's grey, but not raining – and it'll be much greyer still if you stop in all day under my feet. So go on, wrap up and see if your play'll make the day grin!'

Poorly Boy stared at Nelly, shocked at her skills as a ventriloquist from the tray as it landed gently like a flying saucer, doing a slow turn above the drainer. That was it then, adjudged his nose as it came down like a gavel and his chin and palm parted in agreement with the decision, fingers drumming them off with a brief march on his cheek that lasted but a second before they did so.

'Right Mum, good idea, and seeing as it's yours, you can be boss of packing us up for what Nelly decided the other day would be a good idea next time we hadn't one, and you had the idea we should have. I'll go get some grass for sandwiches and you fill a bottle. Lemon, please - the team likes that as well, so we won't have to come back till we've caught one!'

This led to a few questions in Sue's mind that she was going to raise, when she found herself about to address the open door to the garden. But Poorly Boy wasn't long gone and Sue got the chance to raise them. She put the fresh grass cuttings, a mere three weeks old, between six slices of bread and margarine.

'Little Sheeps and Daddy Springy don't like wet grass, but if it's dry, you can damp some for Baby Kenneth as he likes it soggy.'

'Why am I doing this, Poorly Boy?' This was Sue's first, and not unreasonable, question.

Poorly Boy gave her the 'you-must-know' look we use on people whose ignorance amazes us. He handed her - with scrupulously undried, five-year-old washed/unwashed hands - another paw load of yummy, only just beginning to rot, compost off the table's edge, where he'd dumped it from the garden; the paws involved belonging to Little Sheeps and Daddy Springy.

'You're doing it, Mum, because Nelly, being a nurse, is wondering why all grown-ups and far too many bit - grown-ups are scared of calories. You are, and watch one every time you spot it on a box of eats, as if it's going to eat you - and all them people on telly and on magazine pages do, counting every one they see. You're all afraid of them and Nelly wants to find out why.'

Sue, all at once, found herself giving the answers - but she was aware of doing it oddly; almost in a defensive panic. 'It's because they put weight on us - and weight where we don't want it.' She'd regrets even before the end. Poorly Boy had led her to the hunter's pit and shoved her in for Nelly, her staunchest ally even before Ben - to desert her and put the net over Poorly Boy's pit. Sue started to squirm at the bottom of it as Poorly Boy stared one of his 'pity-the-poor-fool' stares - first at Nelly, to see if she'd got the same stare as him - and then at Sue, who knew she was that poor fool awaiting the pit's filling in.

Poorly Boy commenced shovelling. 'Oh Mum, me and Nelly's surprised you didn't think of it too, well as us.'

Oh God, thought Sue, *not the highchair.*

Now this highchair dated back to Poorly Boy's babyhood, all those many five years ago. He'd never let Mum and Dad remove it from its domineering hold on the kitchen corner and at times of great danger to the nation - or his pocket money for being naughty, Garden Shed Infirmary, Baby Kenneth's tooth, or a pending world shortage of cottage cheese cartons - he'd pompously instate it at its rightful head of table. From here, swinging (just enough for effect, but not enough to upend it) with one foot on the first support on the first rung, and the other sort of dangling hypnotically in air slightly, he'd give the oration on whatever threat was impending.

'You can't blame the calories - that's one thing ...' Sue interrupted bravely here, attempting to suppress the next shovelful. 'I'm well aware of that, Poorly Boy; it's we who tend to eat too many of them.' Her voice was rather lacking in patience as opposed to Poorly Boy's still patiently talking to a fool in a pit – leg still beating air like a subdued tom-tom before the cook pot Sue was about to face. With the assembled team on highchair tray before her, (less Nelly; still undecided to get Sue out or join the cannibals) Poorly Boy then dragged Sue firewood-wards.

'Mummy, Mummy,' he began, 'then if you know you eat too many, why do it? Why do it when you know it only gets them even madder and they'll scare you even more?'

Sue, cowering in the pit bottom, looked at him, expressionless. 'They aren't nasty, born that way - oh no, it's that you and all them people who eats calories gets 'em real uptight because you eat them. If you leave them alone and eat proper food instead, leaving the little calories to get on and eat whatever calories eat, they too can have a happy time of their lives and have babies and get married after, just like what we do.'

By this time, Sue was almost pleased to give up the fight and throw herself into the cook pot - so she did.

'But Poorly Boy, all food contains calories. Only water has none.'

'That's because they can't swim, Mum. Fact, there's a starting for you because you can teach them - just smile and say, 'Look, we know we've been cruel to you all these years, but now we isn't going to hurt you poor fings no more - and to prove it, we will show you how to doggy-paddle and not be put off by water any more, or have to go the long way round puddles. Think about it, Mum.'

Sue was getting hotter. She remembered her school day science - a bit - and how a calorie was a sort of measure. Something about raising temperature through one gram of water for some obscure reason. Or was it how to raise one gram to the water's surface? Whatever, she did know they could be fattening if you ate too many and all food and drink contained them, other than water, because they couldn't swim. She realised her head ached and she was becoming a little confused.

Poorly Boy put more wood on the cooking fire. 'They're in food, Mum, cos they dig wiv their sharp teeth, a way in to try escaping from you. They don't want to fight because they're only small; so small you need a microscope to see them bigger than what they are. But they are very brave for their size - so if you touch them in nastiness, it's only natural they'll bite back, isn't it? Which brings me back to where I started.'

Sue felt she might be about done on both sides as well. All it remained then, was for Poorly Boy to start to start carving. 'Leave them alone, Mum, that's my advice to you and all who hurts 'em out there and then you won't even notice they're about.' Poorly Boy left off swinging from the judgement chair and one-legged it across to the compost sandwiches. 'Take this, Mum.' His tone was biblical and all sermons on rocks. 'See,' he said with a flourishing hand, 'it don't bite because there's no calories round it. They knew all along Little Sheeps and Daddy Springy weren't going to hurt them - and that's how I've taught you, you won't never hurt them. They sense it, see Mum. So when they'd finished playing on the grass and the bread (those who hadn't already jumped off when you chopped and margarined, they skipped off hand in hand, and were singing so sweet you couldn't hear them, to play elsewhere. They didn't need to hide inside the bread or grass by burrowing through the surface wiv those same teeth you used to be - before today - scared stiff of. Do you understand how silly you've been, Mummy?'

Nelly unexpectedly fell forwards in some milk Poorly Boy had spilt on the tray, seemingly days before breakfast. Though this was small comfort to Sue, who felt her pink, betrunked saviour had arrived too late, at least what was left of her might still be pulled free from out the pot by the young elephantess.

'Well, Nelly obviously doesn't agree with you for one, Poorly Boy. She's just seen a calorie about to attack her, and maybe even me, in that spilt milk there, and has jumped on it to trunk and squash it!' Sue felt better for this - if only for a moment.

Poorly Boy righted Nelly. *Unduly roughly,* thought Sue.

'Not at all,' he said after a moment's contemplation of the scene before him.

Sue saw the wave of his brain's brainwave, cheerfully waving at her from the glittering windows of Poorly Boy's brown eyes.

'No Mum - wrong again. Nelly's turned thirsty wiv all your talking - and she's not scared of calories neither, so she knows there won't be any hiding from her in that milk and they'll all have gone off playing safely from round it when they saw she's thirsty. They'll work wiv you if you work wiv them.'

Everyone heard the day had decided to have its mind made up for it by itself and rain heavily, if no one was interested in a calorie hunt outside. So Poorly Boy called the whole thing off, and leaving Little Sheeps and Daddy Springy to eat their tasty sandwiches on the table, after the safari he decided to help Mum wash up the pots from breakfast and the hunting expedition just successfully carried out.

'Look at this porridge pan!' he giggled. 'It's gone all messy wiv leaving too long. It looks as if some ... what do you call them? Oh, cannonballs or somefing's been cooking calories in it. I wonder if they found them fattening, Mum?'

There came to Sue's imagination, the image of a friendly little savage grinning up at her.

PRINCESS SUGAR
Patricia Green

It all began in the summer when my mum and I used to sunbathe in the back garden. Princess Sugar used to come round wanting a fuss - she already belonged to someone else but that didn't stop her from coming round. Then one day, Princess Sugar was given to my mum to keep and to look after. If you haven't guessed yet, Princess Sugar was a young cat. She had emerald-green eyes with a sweet small face which was white, with different shades of brown on her body. As the story goes, Princess Sugar was no ordinary cat; she would get up to things other cats wouldn't do.

At dinner time, when my brother was at the table, Princess Sugar would sit near him, waiting for bits of food. When she didn't get any food from him, she knew my mum would throw bits to her. Princess Sugar would do this every day. She had her own cat food, but she insisted she wanted pork chops, ham, chicken, pies; she used to love gravy with most things.

Another thing Princess Sugar would do was drink out of a flowered cup. She would do this when Mum went to bed. Princess Sugar wouldn't drink water from her bowl and she didn't sleep in her own bed - she had to sleep with Mum on her bed. In the middle of the night she would have a drink of water from her flowered cup. Mum and Princess Sugar had their water in different cups. Mum had a lid on hers.

Another side to Princess Sugar was that she got in bad moods and growled at you first; that was a warning not to touch her again. If you did touch her again, she would put her paw out and scratch you, but she did tell you first when she'd had enough. Princess Sugar also did this when she was being combed. Princess Sugar was all right for a while; my mum loved her.

During the day, in winter, Princess Sugar would lay close to the radiator, on the kitchen table, listening to music. She would also sit looking in the window when she was outside, waiting for someone to let her in. Princess Sugar could also stand with one paw in the air.

Princess Sugar did have a friend, he was a prince. Sandy and white in colour, he was nothing like Princess Sugar, but they got on well together. His name was Thomas. Prince Thomas got sick one Christmas; he was very old and he died. Prince Thomas is in Heaven now with all the other cats that have died.

Princess Sugar was alone, but she would never forget Prince Thomas. Princess Sugar wouldn't have wanted her friend to suffer any more. She was happy and remembered the good times spent with Prince Thomas.

Solved
Audrey A Allocca

Meg couldn't wait to meet Anna in the playground at break. As soon as the bell rang she ran out of class and down to the huts to wait. 'Guess what?' she said as soon as Anna arrived. 'Jamie says there's an old witch living in the cave; you can see her from the stile.'

'How does he know? Has he seen her?'

'He says so. Says she wears black clothes and you can see her moving about amongst the rocks, collecting things for her spells and then she just fades into the rocks like magic, so you can't find her.'

'Sounds creepy to me,' said Anna. 'Come on, let's go and play, the bell will go soon.'

All through the rest of the lessons that day, Anna thought about the strange old woman and the mystery surrounding the big cave.

On the way home that afternoon, Anna suddenly said, 'I don't believe Jamie, I think he is just trying to frighten you because you are a girl, but I'll show him. I'll go there and see for myself.'

'What if there is a witch?' asked Meg. 'She may cast a spell on you.'

'That's just my point,' said Anna. 'Why didn't she cast a spell on Jamie and his friends, turn them all into stone or something? It's because he is just trying to frighten you, that's why. There is no such person and I'm going to prove it!'

Eventually Anna persuaded Meg that they ought to go and see for themselves after school one day.

They had planned to go after school today because there wouldn't be any homework, and Mum wouldn't be surprised when they changed into old clothes and went off on their bikes.

They left their bikes by the hedge, climbed over the stile and started up the track as soon as possible. It wound steeply up the hill towards the mouth of the cave. It seemed never-ending. The only signs of life were the occasional sheep droppings, but there was that certain something which made the girls want to see inside. It stayed light until about 9pm in the evenings, but nevertheless, just in case, they had brought their torches - they were sure to need them inside.

'Where's your torch?' asked Anna.

'Here, in my pocket,' replied Meg.

'We'd better use just one in case the batteries go.' Anna switched hers on and they went in.

It was cold and dark inside, and it took a while for their eyes to adjust to the dim light. Meg shivered. 'I don't like it,' she said, and a little voice echoed, *I don't like it, I don't like it.* Meg grabbed Anna in fright.

'Don't be silly, listen, it's us,' and a little voice said, *It's us, it's us, it's us.*

Not wholly convinced, Meg held on to Anna and gingerly they made their way forward. The only other sound, apart from their own footsteps, being the constant trickle of water seeping in from the hills and running down the rocks, forming stalactites and stalagmites.

As the ledge narrowed, they had to proceed singly, pressing themselves back against the damp rocks in case they fell. 'I don't like it,' said Meg. *Don't like it, don't like it,* said the little voice.

Anna shone the torch round the walls. They both screamed and, in her fright, she dropped the torch! There, in the opening, had been a gnarled face with a long, pointed nose. Their screams echoed round the cave eerily and they could hear the torch rolling further away into the darkness.

'Give me your torch, quick!' said Anna.

With trembling fingers, Meg did so. Holding tight to one another, Anna pointed the torch in the same direction and switched it on. They couldn't believe their eyes; no face, no opening, nothing. 'Must have been a trick of the light,' she said, but Meg was not so sure and was all for going home. 'Oh come on, we've come this far, let's just look here,' said Anna.

Reluctantly Meg followed, straining her ears, quite convinced that they were being followed. She was sure she could hear something fairly close behind and whispered to her sister that she thought they were being followed, and a faint little voice said, *Followed, followed.* The great problem was, if they were being followed, they couldn't really go back. 'We're trapped,' said Meg and the mocking little voice confirmed, *Trapped, trapped.*

By mutual agreement, they again began to edge forward and eventually found themselves in quite a wide opening, still quite wet, but with a flat, sandy base where they were able to walk together. On the far side, two little tunnels led off in opposite directions. 'Now where?' said Meg.

'I think we are going round in a circle and if we go right, we'll come back to the entrance of the cave,' said Anna.

So it was agreed that they would follow the path to the right. Holding hands, they set off again and soon, once again found themselves in a fairly wide opening with yet more tunnels leading off. Anna ran the torch round so they could see each one more clearly and, to their horror, leading to one were footprints and, even more strange, whoever it was had no shoes as their toes were clearly imprinted in the soft wet sand. They stood rooted to the spot, trembling with both fear and cold. Somewhere, a stone dislodged and rattled down, eventually falling into some water with a little plop. Their instinct was to run, but which way? The footprints had come from right to left and gone into that tunnel, so was there a way out through either of those? Where did the one in the middle go? Why didn't this person wear shoes? Would they have to wade through water? There was only one set of footprints, but did anyone else live here? They were very frightened now and just wanted to go home.

Cautiously, they made their way towards the right hand tunnel, hardly daring to breathe in case whoever it was came back. It was very dark inside and in their haste they stumbled on the slippery stones. There was also a strange smell. The further they went, the stronger the smell became.

'I wonder what it is?' whispered Meg.

'I don't know, but I think we'll find out quite soon,' replied Anna and again, that mocking little voice said, *Soon, soon.*

They were aware that the nearer they got to the smell, the warmer it became and, emerging into yet another quite large opening, there was a dying fire with a black pot suspended over it and, on the ground, bunches of leaves and flowers.

'It's a witch doing spells,' said Meg. *Doing spells, doing spells,* said the voice.

'Quick, someone's coming,' said Anna, pushing Meg into the nearest tunnel and turning off the torch. They trembled with fear as the shuffling came nearer and nearer, a light flickered eerily on the opposite wall and a dark figure appeared carrying a lantern. They watched, hardly daring to breathe as whoever it was shuffled over to the pot, poured some water in and gave it a stir with a big stick. Suddenly, the figure turned towards them and came shuffling past into a nearby tunnel, returning a few minutes later with some little bottles into which the liquid from the black pot was poured, and then little corks put in. The vapour from the hot liquid drifted into where they were hiding and Meg sneezed.

The dark figure whirled round, shining the flickering lamp into the opening. 'Caught you!' she screamed. 'Spying on me, trying to steal my remedies! Who sent you? You'll pay for this!' and she wagged a bony finger menacingly at them.

Both girls were trembling with fear, never had they seen someone so angry.

'Oh please, Ma'am,' stammered Anna, 'we weren't stealing or spying, we came to see the stalactites and stalagmites and got lost and can't find our way out.'

She peered at them, unsure whether to believe them or not, sucking noisily on her yellowed teeth.

'We thought you were doing spells, so we hid,' said Meg.

The old woman chuckled. 'Oh no, no, I'm no witch, though folks round here seem to think I am. If you must know, I make ointments and medicines from herbs, from recipes handed down from my mother and her mother before her. My family have been in these hills for years. They all know old Mary and her cures for aches and pains, and where to find me in the square on market day.'

'So you're like a doctor then?' said Anna.

'Yes, I suppose you could call me that. My father was a herbalist and known as the Medicine Man.'

What's that smell?' asked Meg. 'It made me sneeze.'

'Oh it will, it's my cold cure, clears the head does that. Just a few drops on your hankie or on some boiling water and breathe it in and your cold disappears, just like that.'

'You're awfully clever,' said Anna. 'Do you live here in this cave all alone?'

'Questions, questions,' said the old woman. 'You children are all the same, but no, I work here with the herbs that grow wild on the hillside and the minerals that are in the spring water. Now that's all I'm telling you. I've told you too much already.'

'But where do you live?' persisted Anna. 'It's so cold in here, and you haven't any shoes.'

The old lady laughed. 'Bless you child, you are a little worrier. I live in a little cottage and don't wear my shoes in here as it can be very slippery. Now no more questions, off you go!'

'Please can you show us how to get out? We don't know which way to go.'

'So you can find my secret cave again, I suppose?'

'Oh no, we won't tell anyone,' they said.

'Come along then, where is home?'

'White Post Farm, but we've left our bikes by the stile and have to get back to where we came in.'

The old lady led them along several passages and eventually they came out onto the hillside. To their right they could see the track they had climbed earlier, and the stile. They thanked her and, promising her they would see her at the market, started off down the hill. When they looked back, she'd gone.

At long last it was market day and two excited little girls couldn't wait to get to the square to prove they hadn't been dreaming. Sure enough, there was their old lady, sitting with her basket. Lots of people were milling round, asking advice, buying medicines and ointments from her. Auntie bought some hand cream and something to rub into Uncle Jack's bad back. As promised, the girls didn't tell anyone about the cave and the old lady just smiled when she saw them.

Later, when they were home, Meg said, 'What do you think we should say if Jamie says anything else about the cave?'

'Just say your aunt said it is haunted and you've got to stay away.'

SAM'S SPACE ADVENTURE
Hazell Dennison

Sam had enjoyed his school holiday and had been playing with his friends from school. They had been fishing for tiddlers in a nearby stream. Now he was home and hungry for tea.

After tea, he had watched television, but now he had fallen fast asleep.

'Come on, sleepyhead,' said his mother, nudging him awake. 'Time for bed.'

Sam stretched and yawned, climbed the stairs, put on his pyjamas and rolled into bed. Soon he was asleep again, but during the night, a bright, powerful light shone through his bedroom window. He quickly woke up, rubbed his eyes and, stumbling, made his way to look out of the window. He couldn't believe his eyes. 'It can't be,' he said out loud, rubbing his eyes yet again in disbelief.

In the darkness, he could see a spaceship, dome-shaped and lights blazing away so brightly. He was excited, but also a little scared. Putting on his slippers and dressing gown, he went to open the back door. He crept nearer and nearer, hiding behind a bush to get a better view.

Suddenly, a door came down from the spacecraft and a figure appeared in a silver suit and helmet, muttering in a foreign language. Sam edged forward and the spaceman caught sight of him and beckoned for him to follow.

By this time Sam was quite excited, but would he be safe? He could see other spacemen through the windows of the spacecraft, all dressed in the same silver spacesuits.

Very slowly he followed the spaceman into the craft. They all seemed very friendly and he felt he could trust them. One of the spacemen came forward carrying a silver space helmet and gave it to Sam to put on, then he pointed towards the sky.

'Yes please,' said Sam, 'I would like to go for a ride in your spaceship.'

Sam watched as the spacemen pressed lots of buttons and controls, then the doors closed again. Up high they flew amongst the clouds, passing the stars and the moon, spinning, twisting and turning so fast.

But all too soon it was over and the spacecraft landed in the same spot as when Sam had first seen it; in the meadow near his back garden.

'Thank you,' replied Sam, 'I will never forget my space adventure.'

The spacemen shook Sam's hand and let him keep the lovely, shiny, silver space helmet. Now the spacecraft took off again, leaving Sam waving goodbye to his space friends.

Tiptoeing back into his house so he wouldn't wake anyone, he took off his space helmet and got back into bed, falling fast asleep.

In the morning he thought he'd been dreaming about everything, until he sat up in bed and there, on his bedside table, was the gleaming silver space helmet. He was so eager to tell his friends and parents about his space adventure, but then, who would believe him?

A Wonderful Life
(For my great niece, Molly Tame)
Gerard Allardyce

He was bought for my eighth birthday. My mother and father decided it would be nice if I could have a pet that would be simple to look after. In truth, this would only be at weekends.

Mum and Dad decided to buy the budgie in an old style pet shop in Crawley. It was April 1961 and I had just started attending Westminster Cathedral Choir School the previous January.

They were both in the shop. 'Come on, Rene, I am fed up. Choose any bird and let's get home. Gerard's quite involved with his electric train set.'

'I am going to buy this bird,' my mother said, with a glint in her eye. 'He is a feisty bird with unusual cobalt-blue colouring.'

A sales assistant served my mother and put the bird in a little cardboard box. 'Trill is the best seed to use to feed a budgerigar.'

My mother replied, 'Now, I think I know that. What is your name?'

'Charlotte.'

'Well Charlotte, besides Trill and cuttlefish, budgies also like greenery in the diet to help keep them well. They live longer; my grandmother always gave hers linnet groundsel.'

'Can you give budgies groundsel, Madam?'

'Oh yes, you find the plant in most gardens and growing wild on commons and in parks, as well as in woodland and near streams. Budgies also like bits of lettuce. By the way, Charlotte, how old is this little bird?'

'It's been four or five weeks since he hatched.'

'And how much will he be?'

'Just one pound, Madam.'

'He's a bargain for that price.'

'I see you have bought one of our nice little cages, I am sure that this bird will be well looked after and live a long life in your care.'

'Thank you, Charlotte,' and my mother and father left the shop with the little blue budgie. 'Oh, he's tweeting,' my mother cried happily.

'What shall we name him?' asked my father.

'Georgie, I think, and I shall teach him to talk. My brother's bird can say, 'Bobby Stephen', we will do better than that.'

And so it was. The little bird found his new home in the bay window of our house.

I came downstairs; Dad was listening to his vintage 1947 wireless. 'Shh, don't make a lot of noise Gerard, your little bird is sitting on the bottom of his cage. He is very nervous and I have found in the last half hour that he likes the light programme.'

This was my first real acquaintance with Georgie and I was due back at boarding school in a few days. The day was Saturday and after breakfast, I had a chat with Mum about the prospects of teaching Georgie to talk.

'My grandmother had a mynah bird which talked beautifully,' my mother said. 'The secret, Gerard, is that you talk nicely to him at the corner of his cage for about an hour a day. Now obviously, you repeat his name, Georgie, kiss, Georgie, kiss, Georgie. You must be patient, Gerard, he is a young bird, not long out of the egg. When you start to teach him to talk he will not tweet, but listen.'

This proved sound advice and, in-between playing with my Hornby Dublo electric train set and battery-powered robot, I talked to this loveable little bird.

When I was at the choir school, my sister, Margaret, sent me pictures of Georgie in her letters. Mrs O'Sullivan, the maths teacher, thought it very amusing when I opened the envelope because feathers flew everywhere!

Dear Gerard,
 Here are some of Georgie's feathers; he is moulting at the moment.
  Your loving sister,
   Margaret.

That first summer, like every summer that followed, was the time when Georgie moulted. It was because of the heat, but I said to Mum, he must never be allowed to end up looking like an oven-ready turkey.

'Now that's silly,' Mum said.

Georgie was now about four months old and had become a fluent talker. Apart from 'Kiss me Georgie', which we had all taught him, my mother had taught him the beginning of a nursery rhyme which began, 'Georgie Porgie, pudding and pie, kissed ...' but the dear little bird had not learnt to say any more than that. Dad considered it time to find Georgie a mate.

'Oh no, don't do that,' Margaret exclaimed in alarm to Father. 'Budgerigars are territorial birds, like robins. At school we introduced a female bird into a cage with a male and overnight they killed each other, you should have seen the blood!'

Mother was cross. 'Margaret, please. that's enough. That's distasteful talk in front of a little boy. Budgies killing each other indeed!'

This was one of many memorable moments in the sixteen-year life of Georgie the budgie. One other endearing memory was Mum going up to the cage with a piece of groundsel and observing Georgie with a smile as he ate the yellow bud off the plant.

The seasons came and went, as did my time at school, leading up to teacher training college.

'You've failed at college,' my father said, with obvious disappointment, but at least my budgie still shrilled a greeting to his long-lost pal.

Mum and Dad moved away from Crawley and our home changed.

One day, Georgie flew a couple of feet outside the kitchen door, into the garden. Mother was distraught. 'Now, you are not going to fly away, we would never see you again and we love you far too much to allow that, Georgie,' and she threw a tea towel over the bird and safely carried him back to his cage.

In the summer, Georgie had a little plastic bath attached to his cage, with a mirror. 'All budgies are vain and love to preen themselves and look at themselves,' said Mum.

In 1974, Mum and Dad drove to the Brecon Beacons, towing a caravan. Georgie was in his cage in the caravan. He loved the journey, he chirped and tweeted and said, 'Kiss me Georgie' and sang 'Georgie Porgie, pudding and pie'.

I was away in the summer of 1975 when Margaret and her young son, Andrew, came to visit Mum and Dad. Margaret thought something was wrong the night before, as Georgie's feathers were all puffed up and he was balancing on one foot on his swing.

Margaret got up to make the morning tea, whilst Mum, Dad and little Andrew were still in bed. She decided to check on our dear little friend, who had brought us all such pleasure over the years. She found him on the bottom of the cage with his little claws in the air, but he was still tweeting. He was no longer able to perch and Margaret wondered if it was worth taking him to the vet in the village. Mum and Dad were so upset.

'We all love him, but he is Gerard's bird,' Mum said.

Margaret said, 'I'll stay home while you and Dad take Georgie to the vet.'

'I think that's wise,' said Dad. 'We don't want to upset young Andy.'

Georgie was taken to the vet in the same little cardboard box he had arrived in sixteen years earlier. The vet assured my parents, 'You have looked after him very well, Mr and Mrs Allardyce, in effect he has lived the equivalent of three budgie lives, but now I know what I must do.'

And so it was at an end, the saga of a loving pet who had brought everyone so much pleasure. There were tears streaming from my mother's eyes and a young assistant made her a cup of tea.

'On to pastures new, Irene,' my father comforted her. 'I'll make a fish pond in the back garden, next to the sunflowers.'

And so it was that the grandchildren from Australia came to visit and went fishing. Soon, Mum and Dad's pond was full of not only goldfish, but also small trout! Mum and Dad's niece, Carolyn, came to stay too.

Mum told her, 'Gerard's become engaged to a lovely girl called Georgina …' and on that note, I shall end my story.

BETTY'S MIRROR
Danielle Eyres

The playground can be the biggest battlefield of your life. When all you have to fight with is who you are, be proud of it and use it as your armour.

Betty Booley was enduring another achingly long day at Richlee Secondary School. As she stood at the edge of the playing field, alone, eating an egg mayonnaise sandwich her mother had lovingly prepared for her, she felt the first familiar sting of a stone on the back of her leg.

'Oi! Fatty!' came the taunting voice of Lionie Crabshaw. 'Should you really be eating lunch? Wouldn't a diet be better for you?'

'Oh, don't be cruel, Lionie!' shouted Mona Sagget. 'She's obviously on a diet ... chocolate for breakfast, biscuits for lunch and cream cakes for tea, can't you see?'

Cackles of laughter exploded behind her, whilst large dollops of tears fell into Betty's egg sandwich. She refused to give them the pleasure of seeing her crying, but at the same time, she knew what was coming next. It was the same almost every lunchtime, Lionie's gang always managed to find her. There would be more pebbles thrown, more jibes and rhymes and then they would circle around her and snatch her lunch, saying it was for her own good. Today was no different. As they came up behind her, chanting, *'Betty Booley, fell in a pool-ey of ice cream, ice cream ...'* she was reminded of something she had seen on television when a deer was being hunted by a pack of wolves. There was no escape. She stuffed the rest of her sandwich into her lunch box, pushed the lunch box back into her rucksack and was just starting back towards the school hall when *slam,* she fell to the ground. Lionie's friend, Emma Bunce, had tripped her up.

'Oops, sorry Big Betty, didn't mean to cause an earthquake!' said Emma in a sugary voice.

Betty was winded and couldn't breathe, let alone reply. As she felt her rucksack whipped off her back and saw the three girls dance victoriously away, she felt sick deep in the pit of her stomach. Her hands stung, blood oozed from her lip where she had bitten it whilst falling, and the front of her school uniform was splattered with mud and wet grass.

Her music exam was due to start in fifteen minutes and she looked a complete mess. On top of that, her music piece was in her rucksack. Betty loved singing and had been practising for months, but today was turning into one of the worst school days of her life and she had no one to talk to about it. If she told a teacher, as they were encouraged to do if they were being bullied, the teacher would tell the headmistress, who just so happened to be Lionie's mum, and Betty felt for sure that she would not be believed. If she told her mum, the end result was bound to be the same, because her mum would want to go straight to Mrs Crabshaw. So, after collecting a spare shirt from the school secretary and embarrassingly being given her rucksack, which had been handed in, torn and minus her lunch, Betty made her way, heavy-hearted, to the music rooms.

The music exam was actually a thin shaft of sunlight on a stormy day for Betty Booley. Singing was her passion, not only because she liked it, but because she was truly gifted. Her voice was powerful, yet sweet, and she had an amazing range that could make low notes sound like the rush of a deep river and high notes sound like a skylark dancing in the air. She closed her eyes from the horrors of the day and, with the only other sound being the accompanying piano from her classmate, Juliette, Betty's heart was lifted and she was somewhere far away, singing for her soul.

Her eyes were still closed at the end of the piece when Juliette interrupted her. 'Betty, you were amazing! God, I wish I could belt it out like that!'

'Thanks, Juliette, but it wouldn't have sounded half as good without your piano playing.'

Betty had always hoped that she and Juliette could be friends, but Juliette was a peripheral member of Lionie's 'cool gang' and she was only nice to Betty when no one else was around. Betty knew that behaviour like that was a poor sign of friendship.

When Betty arrived home and her mum asked about the music exam, Betty only half smiled when she replied, 'Good, well yeah, good. I got an 'A' for the singing.'

'Wow, Betty! That's excellent, you're going to be famous one day, I know it! Want some tea and cake to celebrate?'

'No thanks, Mum, actually I'm not feeling so great, do you mind if I go to my room for a bit?'

'Of course not, darling, probably the excitement of the day, eh?'

Betty climbed the stairs and went into the bedroom and shut the door, biting her lip and fighting back the tears again. Their house was in a small row of cottages in the fishing village of Port Mannion and from her window sill, Betty could gaze out to sea. She watched the heavy October clouds rolling in like a deep, dark blanket of despair and she wished she had someone to chat to.

She switched on her radio, sat down in front of her dressing table and opened the bottom drawer, which was stuffed full of her favourite treats for unhappy moments. This, considered Betty, was a truly unhappy moment, most deserving of at least three chocolate bars and perhaps a mini cake too. As she peeled open a wrapper, she stopped and took a hard look at herself in the mirror. A large, tear-stained face stared back: big, brown, sad eyes, trembling, wide lips and podgy hands holding a chocolate bar that would just prove Lionie's gang right. As she put down the chocolate and stared once more at her reflection it happened; the moment that would change Betty's life.

Something in the reflection moved. The bedroom door swung open and Betty expected to see her mother carrying a tea tray, but instead she saw the reflection of a small, dark-haired girl, wearing a red dress. She came right up to the dressing table and stood at Betty's shoulder.

'Hello, Betty!' she said with a large grin. 'I'm here to help you see yourself. It's very important that you tell me what you can see.'

Betty was transfixed. She wasn't dreaming, but she didn't dare turn around in case the girl disappeared. 'Well,' Betty replied, 'I see me, Big Betty, Betty who causes an earth tremor when she falls, who can't be anyone's friend because they get embarrassed by me. I see fat face, fat fingers and fat fingers holding more chocolate because they're right ... I must deserve to be called those names.' Betty looked up.

'No, Betty,' said the girl gently, 'this is why you need to learn more about yourself. What I see is a flower waiting to open and at the moment she can't because there are too many prickly thorns blocking the sunlight.'

'Well, if you mean Lionie and her friends, you're right, but they bully me and there isn't anything I can do.'

'Rubbish!' said the girl in the red dress. 'You can learn to stand up for yourself, learn to say no and to be proud of who you are. You like singing, don't you?'

'Love it!' exclaimed Betty, her face lighting up.
'Now look again at your reflection.'
Betty looked and was truly surprised at the difference.
The girl in the red dress smiled, 'Now I see the real Betty, a gorgeous smile, sparkling dark eyes, olive skin and a figure like Jennifer Lopez!'
Betty's grin widened. 'Well, maybe,' she murmured.
'Of course, maybe!' said the girl. 'Now that you've learnt something about yourself, use what makes you feel good to ooze that in confidence. Those bullies will hate it and it's the best weapon you've got against them, believe me ...'
'Really?' Betty was unsure, especially when she thought back to the events that lunchtime.
The girl turned to walk away. 'Really, you're Beautiful Betty, not Big Betty, so give it a go ...'
And with that she was gone. Betty turned, but the door was shut; she didn't know whether it was imagined or real, but she felt different inside. Betty sat breathless for a while. The first thing she did was to empty her drawer full of 'needy-snacks' into the bin. She didn't need them! She replaced them with meaningful, 'feel-good' objects - her music notation, shells from a holiday, photos of her cousin and her favourite DVDs. The girl in the red dress had been right, but Betty was worried that her confidence wouldn't last through the next few days of school.

'Oi! Big Bum Betty!' came the shrill shriek of Lionie's voice the following day in music class. 'Juliette says you can sing ... a bit of a Pavarotti, eh? Bettybotti! Ha! So tell me, Fat Bettybotti, what are you kindly giving me for lunch today?'
'Actually, nothing,' Betty started, assertively. 'You seem to be jealous that I can sing and I've been told that my 'botti' is more of a J-Lo 'botti' than a 'Pavabotti', so get lost! Go and torture someone else, because I haven't got time for your games, OK?' Betty was quivering inside, but it felt good to answer back.
Lionie, however, was shaking with surprise and rage. How dare Big Betty speak to her like that, and in front of her girls? Then she noticed Juliette smiling. Lionie turned on Juliette, 'Well, Ginger Mouse, aren't you going to say something to that fat cow, or are you the pathetic creep

that I always thought you were, just following me around because you haven't got any friends either?'

So Juliette turned to Betty, but having seen Lionie in her true light, she wasn't going to stand for it anymore. 'Betty ... you ... you ... you sure can sing. You probably will end up in the charts, like J-Lo!'

Lionie almost went purple and shook her head of blonde curls violently. 'Juliette, you're banned from the gang!'

'OK, fine, Lionie,' Juliette replied. 'I was sick of your cruel games anyway.' Juliette picked up her bag and marched over to sit beside Betty. 'Mind if I join you?' she asked.

'Course not!' said Betty with a smile that was growing more confident by the minute.

At that point they were interrupted by Miss Devonish, the music teacher. 'Children, we have a new pupil today, please make Rianna welcome.'

A dark-haired girl in a red dress stood at the front of the class and smiled. Betty had to look twice; the girl looked so similar to the girl in the mirror and Betty, who didn't really believe in strange things happening, felt that if this wasn't strange, then it had to be for a reason.

'Juliette, Betty, Martha, I wonder if you'd mind showing Rianna around, please?' Miss Devonish asked.

'Of course not!' Juliette said loudly on behalf of them.

Days of friendship turned into years of friendship between the girls. As they sat on the playing field one lunchtime, the week before they left school, Juliette remarked, 'School was so dull really, I mean, do you think we actually learnt anything useful? I don't.'

The others agreed, but Betty felt differently, 'Yes, I do think we learnt a lot, about ourselves mainly. We learnt that we can grow as people, not just grow up, and we can learn to love ourselves and others, for who they are, and I reckon that's a lesson worth learning.'

Betty knew that it still wouldn't be easy, and the bullies would always be out there, but she was fully equipped with knowing how to be herself and for her, life was just beginning.

MRS PRICKLES' TRAVELS
Yvonne Peacock

One morning as the sun was rising, Mrs Prickles went in to wake her babies, Prudence and Patrick. 'Wake up, you two, and get ready to go out. We are going to visit your auntie and it's a long way to walk for two little hedgehogs like you.'

They all had some breakfast and got ready for the journey to see their auntie.

Patrick said, 'How far is it to Auntie's, Mum?'

Mrs Prickles said, 'Well dear, I have only been there once before, but I know it will take a very long time.'

So off they went down the lane, heading for Bluebell Wood. Prudence saw some blackberries in the hedge and stopped to eat some.

'You'll get tummy ache if you eat too many berries,' said Mrs Prickles.

They came to the big gate at the end of the lane. They could see Bluebell Wood.

'Oh Mum, isn't it lovely? It's so blue, and the trees are big,' said Prudence.

'Yes dear, it is lovely, but stay by me, don't wander away,' said Mrs Prickles.

They went under the gate and started to walk through the bluebells.

'Hello there, and where are you going on such a lovely day?' said a little dormouse.

Patrick said, 'We're going to see our auntie; she lives a long way away.'

'Would you like to stay for lunch?' asked the dormouse.

Mrs Prickles said, 'That would be nice, but we have to keep going as it is a long way.'

Walking through the woods, Prudence and Patrick saw lots of animals, birds and insects. When they got to the other side of the woods, there was another big gate to go under. Sitting on the gate was a nymph dressed in pink. Her wings sparkled with gold and silver threads. 'It's a lucky nymph,' said Mrs Prickles.

'Hello,' said the nymph. 'Where are you going on such a lovely day?'

'We are going to see our auntie,' said Patrick.

The nymph said, 'You will have to be very careful as Mrs Fox will be out soon, taking her cubs for a walk. It's getting near their teatime.'

'Thank you, we will get to the river as fast as we can,' said Mrs Prickles. 'Hurry now, you two, don't hang around. Stay with me, we have to cross the road.'

Prudence and Patrick ran across the road behind their mum. It was funny to go on the road as it was all gritty and hard, but they got over safely.

Walking over the grass, they found their way down to the river bank.

'Don't go falling in, as you can't swim,' said Mrs Prickles.

There was a grey heron standing in the shallow water by the river's edge. 'Hello, where are you going on such a lovely day?'

'We are going to see our auntie,' said Prudence.

Patrick said, 'Could you tell us how we get to the other side of the river?'

'Well,' said the heron, 'you will have to go all the way down to the bridge. You will see Mr Frog down in the water by the bridge. He will see you across safely.'

'Thank you,' said Mrs Prickles.

Off they went down to the bridge to find Mr Frog.

'Hello there, and where are you going on such a lovely day?'

'It's Mr Frog,' said Prudence. 'We are going to see our auntie. Can you see us over the bridge to the other side of the river?'

'We will have to hurry, as Mr Owl will be out soon looking for something for his supper,' said Mr Frog.

Over the bridge they went to the other side.

'Thank you,' said Mrs Prickles as she walked down the river bank on the other side.

'Are we nearly there, Mum?' said Patrick.

'Not long now, dear, just down to where you see that big white swan. Your auntie lives in that big old tree in the hedge.'

They walked down the river to the swan.

'Hello, where are you going on such a lovely evening?' said the swan.

'We are going to see our auntie, she lives under that big old tree,' said Prudence.

Waiting at the big old tree was Auntie Pippa Prickles. 'Hello, I am so glad you got here safely,' she said. 'You must come in and have supper, and then we will all go to bed.'

Mrs Prickles, Prudence, Patrick and Auntie Pippa all went to sleep, wrapped up in crunchy dry leaves, all cosy and warm.

A Holiday In Scotland
Elizabeth Love

Jonny and Sara lived with their mother and father in the beautiful little village of Grasmere in the heart of the Lake District. Their grandfather and grandmother lived on a farm near a little place called Ecclefechan on the other side of the border between Scotland and England. The children had visited their grandparents at the farm several times and they were looking forward to going there to stay.

'When you are a bit older,' their mother had told them when they questioned her.

Then Jonny's seventh birthday came round in February and they thought surely they would be allowed to go to Scotland for a holiday. In answer to their entreaties, their mother told them to write to their grandmother and ask her if they could go for their Easter holidays. The reply to their letter was a phone call to their mother saying they were invited to go for a few days at Easter. Sara, who was two years older than Jonny, reminded him about the dyeing of Pasche eggs and subsequent rolling of them on Easter Sunday. It was the first time they had stayed away from home and they were very excited.

Jonny and Sara packed their bags on Wednesday night in readiness for the car coming to collect them the following day. Sara asked her mother if she could take her green silk party dress and was told that she could take it to wear on Easter Sunday. Jonny took his Meccano set. They also took a bag full of onion peelings which their mother had saved for the Pasche egg-making.

They were both looking forward to seeing Marmaduke again, the black and white donkey. Jonny thought he could ride on its back if Sara held the reins and led the way. It had a long black mane and a glossy coat. The first thing they did on arriving was to run down to the paddock.

In another field, there were three mountain sheep with large yellow horns. These had been bought in the Highlands of Scotland and were kept for their especially soft wool. Jonny and Sara gave them names and they christened them Mufty, Tufty and Flora, and they went eagerly down to the field the next morning to see the fascinating animals.

There were also the two pet lambs, which had been brought into the farmhouse kitchen and which had to be fed like babies from a milk bottle. The children watched their grandmother as she held the lamb on her lap, forcing open its mouth with finger and thumb, whilst tipping the bottle with the other hand.

Jonny was captivated. 'Will it ever grow up to be strong, like the lambs in the field?' he asked.

'Oh yes. Two days from now, this little lamb will be fostered by another mother whose lamb has died, and it will grow like all the other lambs,' his grandmother told him. Then she said, 'Tomorrow, you can come with me to feed the hens.'

The henhouse was at the bottom of a field on the edge of a wood. They looked forward to the following day, which was Good Friday.

'Maybe we will see a gorilla,' said Jonny. He had seen a programme about gorillas on television and, like any small seven-year-old boy, he had a vivid imagination.

'There won't be any gorillas,' replied his sister, 'but you might see a badger.'

Sara had been down to the henhouse with her grandmother on another occasion and she had made a short journey into the wood and had discovered a badger sett. She recognized it as such because she had seen badgers on the television and she knew all about their habits.

'How exciting!' cried Jonny. 'I do hope I see a badger in the wood.'

'Well, you will be lucky,' Sara told him. 'They are very shy creatures and usually come out after dark, but they are in a shaded corner beside a stone wall, so there is a chance that you might see one.'

There were reddish-brown Rhode Island hens which laid brown eggs and white Leghorns, that laid white eggs.

'There may be some primroses growing in the wood,' their grandmother told them. 'You could pick some to decorate your Easter eggs.'

Sure enough, after they had helped to collect the eggs out of the nests, they found some primroses. They went further into the wood.

'Follow me,' said Sara, 'and keep every quiet.'

They carried on for a short distance and, creeping forward, they came to where the badgers were.

'Shh,' beckoned Sara and as they waited, they were greeted by two little black and white striped heads which appeared above the ground. Then they were gone again. 'Those would be the babies,' Sara told her brother.

On the way back, they picked some primroses and hurried back to the house to put the flowers into water.

Gathering the eggs that day, Jonny and Sara were prompted to ask about the three nest boxes which they had noticed in the barn, and about the hens which sat there all day long.

'Oh, those are the 'clockers',' they were told. 'They won't lay eggs anymore, so we get three or four pot eggs and put them in the nests under the hens. After a while they will stop clocking and start to lay eggs again!'

Jonny didn't understand why the hen would want to sit there all day, but Sara knew it had something to do with the hen thinking it was hatching out the eggs.

That night they laid all the things out on the kitchen table in readiness for the Pasche egg-making. 'Have you got some newspapers?' Sara asked her grandmother.

'Yes, I've got plenty of newspapers and two colours of string to tie the eggs. That way you will know which eggs are which when they come out of the pan. The white eggs will take the dye best.'

They were each given six white eggs. Their grandmother had another suggestion. 'If you go a little way up the road, you will see some gorse bushes in flower and those will be very good for dyeing your eggs, but be careful and watch the road.'

There were some pieces of coloured cotton material in blues and reds and yellows, and they cut them up into small pieces. In the front garden, they had found some feathery little ferns. Jonny thought it was like the craft class at school, where they made things out of coloured cardboard and felt, and he enjoyed doing things like that. They had everything ready.

'Watch what I do,' Sara instructed as she laid a bed of onion peelings onto a double sheet of newspaper. Jonny copied her. Next she arranged a flower head and a fern and placed the egg in the middle. Jonny copied her again. They each put some peelings, cotton pieces and flowers on top of their eggs and rolled it up inside the paper.

'I don't think I can tie mine,' said Jonny in dismay.

Sara saw him struggling and came to the rescue with the green string. She found that she needed some help as well, and Jonny held the parcel while she tied it with the blue string. In less than an hour they had all twelve parcels ready to go into the very large pan, to be boiled on the stove for fifteen minutes.

They waited eagerly for the eggs to be ready, wondering if the petals and ferns would be imprinted on the eggs. When they had been cooled down with a pan full of cold water, they each opened their respective parcels and were quite surprised with the results. Their grandmother said she would be the judge, and chose Jonny's egg as the winner.

On Easter Sunday morning, the children were out of bed early as it was to be a very special day. Their aunt and uncle and their two young cousins were coming from nearby Glencaple for dinner. Then they were all going on a two and a half mile walk to the neighbouring farm - a route which would take them through some fields and by the river, and past St Mungo's church.

Jonny and Sara were wanting to show off their Pasche eggs. They thought the eggs looked very nice, together with their chocolate ones, arranged in a fancy dish on the farmhouse kitchen window sill.

'I think I am going to leave my best one behind,' said Jonny. 'It would be a pity if it got broken. I want to take it home for Mamma to see.'

'Well in that case, I will leave one too,' said Sara, who secretly thought she had made the best one.

'Can we take Pippa with us on the walk?' asked Jonny. He loved Pippa, the puppy, and had played with her a lot, throwing balls and watching her jump for them.

They set off after dinner and soon came in sight of the first of three stiles. Jonny ran on in front of the rest and reached the stile. He scaled the two stone steps and, standing aloft on the top of the wall, he waved to the other three children who were following with the grown-ups. 'Look at me,' he called.

Pippa climbed after him and then they both jumped down onto the far side and waited for the others to catch up. When they got as far as the second stile, the church came into view. 'I can see the church,' Jonny exclaimed from the vantage point on the top of the wall.

When they got a bit further, they saw the very old church with its steeple, and they peeped inside the half-open door. The interior was decorated with flowers for Easter and was a vision of colour and freshness.

They carried on to the hill behind the church to roll their eggs and oranges. The sticks and stones were a hazard and caused the eggs to break. The game was to see whose eggs could roll the longest without breaking. There was a lot of shouting as the children ran up and down the hill. When they had finished, the whole party sat down on the grass and enjoyed a family picnic. It was quiet and peaceful down by the river, with only the chirping of the birds amongst the trees which were just coming into leaf.

After tea, Uncle William went along the river bank in search of a particular willow tree, in order to make two whistles. He fashioned them with his penknife and gave them to Jonny and Sara.

'How did you do that?' they asked in amazement.

'Well, you see it has to be at the time of year when the sap is in the stem,' they were told. He took a piece of willow and showed them how the bark was peeled away. It had been an exciting afternoon.

On returning home to Grasmere, they were asked how they had enjoyed their visit to Ecclefechan. They showed their mother and father their prize eggs and their handmade whistles, and told them all about their thrilling holiday.

INFORMATION

We hope you have enjoyed reading this book - and that you will continue to enjoy it in the coming years.

If you are interested in becoming a New Fiction author then drop us a line, or give us a call, and we'll send you a free information pack.

Alternatively if you would like to order further copies of this book or any of our other titles, then please give us a call or log onto our website at www.forwardpress.co.uk

**New Fiction Information
Remus House
Coltsfoot Drive
Peterborough
PE2 9JX
(01733) 898101**